THE JUNKYARD DOG

ERIKA TAMAR

A Knopf Paperback
Alfred A. Knopf
New York

In memory of Manon

A KNOPF PAPERBACK PUBLISHED BY ALFRED A. KNOPF, INC.

Library of Congress Cataloging-in-Publication Data
Tamar, Erika.
The junkyard dog / by Erika Tamar.
Summary: With the advice of her stepfather, eleven-year-old Katie takes
on the job of feeding an abused junkyard dog and building it a
doghouse for shelter during the hard winter.
[1. Dogs—Fiction. 2. Pets—Fiction. 3. Stepfathers—Fiction.] I. Title.
PZ7.T159Ju   1995
[Fic—dc20]   94-22368

ISBN 0-679-87057-1 (trade)
0-679-88561-7 (pbk.)

First Knopf Paperback edition: October 1997
Printed in the United States of America
10 9 8 7 6 5 4

THE JUNKYARD DOG

CHAPTER ONE

Katie saw the group of teenage boys gathered in front of Farrow's junkyard on St. Francis Street. She had heard them horsing around from a block away. A gang like that could mean trouble, she thought. But she was only eleven; they wouldn't bother with her. Anyway, they were on the other side of St. Francis. She'd just go on by.

Usually she went home the front way along Grosvenor Avenue, but today she'd decided to take the long way around instead. She'd stayed after school for basketball practice, but it still wasn't six o'clock yet. She made her steps as slow as she could, even though it was cold with the sun almost down. If she *really* took her time, maybe Mom would be home from work already.

Then she wouldn't have to be alone with Jim Grady.

Mom said to keep away from St. Francis Street after dark. That's when the button factory was closed and the sidewalk was deserted except for people going into the Dew Drop bar or the all-night 7-Eleven. The Dew Drop's neon sign was already on, even though it wasn't dark yet. Anyway, Mom worried too much.

Katie walked past a long stretch of pock-marked gray bricks. She couldn't see the river behind all the big buildings, but she could feel the clammy chill coming up from it and she could smell it. The river was why her neighborhood was called the Mud Flats. Way before she was born, even before Mom was born, there was nothing here but muddy banks, and then the city crowded out to the river's edge and they built the projects where Katie lived. Grandma Hattie said it used to be real pretty back when you could see the water.

Now Katie was directly across the street from the teenage boys. They were yelling and pitching stones over the junkyard fence.

And then she heard barking coming from the junkyard. They were throwing stones at a dog!

She hesitated. She didn't *want* to see, but she

couldn't keep herself from crossing the street to look.

A guard dog was fenced in and surrounded by a jumble of used metal parts. The new signs on the chain-link fence said KEEP OUT and BEWARE OF DOG. The dog stood stiff-legged as far back in the yard as he could get, barking hoarsely. He was medium-sized and muddy brown.

Good thing the fence was high, Katie thought; most of the stones didn't make it over. But she saw the terror in the dog's eyes.

She wasn't looking for trouble, but she *had* to say something. "That's mean! Why are you doing that?"

"Just for fun," one boy said. Katie recognized him from the projects.

"To see how tough he is," another answered.

The dog didn't look fierce to Katie. He looked skinny under his matted hair.

Katie bit her lip. Two of the six boys were wearing skull-and-crossbones gang jackets. They could turn on her in a second. She'd better keep quiet and go straight home, she thought.

A stone hit the dog. He yelped in pain.

"Don't!" burst out of Katie. "He can't even run away!"

They kept right on throwing at him.

"Come on, don't. Stop it! Leave him alone."

Seemed like she was invisible and the wind had carried her voice away. No one looked at her or listened, no matter what she said.

She was relieved when they got bored. They went on down St. Francis Street, yelling and wrestling with each other.

Katie could see the dog's ribs sticking out under his fur. He eyed her warily, cringing, with his ears flattened back.

"It's okay," she called. She crouched down. "I won't hurt you."

He didn't trust her. He wouldn't come closer.

Katie thought he might be part terrier. He had pointy ears, a short furry muzzle, and a square body. Whenever Katie dreamed about a dog, she'd picture a cute waggy-tailed puppy like one in the Disney movies. This one was so bedraggled. He was dirty. The bewildered misery in his eyes made her uncomfortable.

Katie stuck her hands deep in her jacket pockets. It was too cold to hang around. She pushed her feet toward the apartment. Mom wouldn't be home yet; it was too early. Jim Grady left before anyone was awake and came home first. He would be there now. She didn't know how to act with him. She could never think of anything to say.

Why did Mom have to get married now, just when everything had been going along okay? Katie didn't mind being home by herself anymore; she'd just settle in and do her homework until Mom came. She was old enough now to get dinner started. They'd been doing fine, just the two of them. Then Jim Grady moved right in last week and everything turned upside down. All of a sudden, Mom was Mrs. Mary Ann Grady and she was still Katie Lawrence. They didn't even have the same name anymore.

Jim Grady was so big. He crowded the apartment. When he sat down, his legs stretched way out and Katie had to be careful not to bump into them. He was a carpenter and he was away most of the day, but his things were around all the time, everywhere: his huge dusty boots, his toolbox, his shaving stuff spilling out of the bathroom cabinet, his toothbrush right there in the cup leaning against hers and Mom's.

Katie used to share the bedroom with Mom. It had Katie's travel posters on the wall and rosy curtains that Mom had made on Grandma Hattie's sewing machine. When Jim Grady came, they moved Katie's bed into a corner of the living room.

He was sitting in the kitchen when Katie came into the apartment, holding the three-paneled wood screen he'd been working on. It had flowers and leaves carved at the top. His tools were spread out on the kitchen table. There was hardly room for Katie to pour a glass of milk.

"School okay today?" he asked.

"Uh-huh." She felt tongue-tied with him. She didn't know what to call him. No one had told her.

"Anything interesting happen?"

Katie shook her head. The junkyard dog floated into her mind, with that bewildered expression in his eyes like he couldn't understand how he'd gotten into such a fix. She wished she'd never seen him. Mom always said what you don't know won't hurt you.

Jim Grady concentrated on the panels. Seemed like he had nothing to say to her, either.

His tools scraped against the wood. The refrigerator hummed. Katie felt a little tickle in her throat.

He had long dark hair pulled back with a rubber band. Did he think he was a rock star or what? Did Mom *like* that?

Finally he spoke. "One more hinge to go." He was looking at the wood, not at her. Was she supposed to answer him?

She sipped at the milk while he screwed in some nails.

He tested the hinges. "Yeah, that should hold good. Come on." He got up and she followed him into the living room, where he set the screen alongside her bed.

"For privacy. It's okay to paste your posters on it."

A bed in the living room wasn't *private,* thought Kate. No three-paneled screen was about to change that.

He looked at her, as if he was expecting something, so she remembered to say thanks.

They both stood staring at the screen. It seemed like forever. Katie's hands dangled at her sides.

Jim cleared his throat. "Your posters, Hawaii, Paris...You want to go there, huh?"

Katie shrugged. She didn't have anything to say about those places. The pictures looked pretty, that was all. She felt stupid.

Finally Mom came home from work. She and Jim hugged so hard that Katie had to look away. Then he led Mom over to the screen with his arm around her shoulders.

Mom ran her finger along the carved part. "That's honest-to-God beautiful. Beautiful!"

"It ain't *that* great, Mary Ann."

"Oh yes it is!" Mom's big smile made her dimples show. "You've got golden hands. Doesn't he, Katie? See, now you've got your own little room!"

Her own room? No way. But she had to smile back, a pretend smile that made her cheeks ache.

At dinner that night, the words blurted right out of Katie. "Mom, Mr. Farrow put a dog in the junkyard!"

"What's he got there that's worth guarding?" Mom said.

"Addicts, they're crazy." Jim Grady took a big heap of mashed potatoes. "They'll steal anything, anytime, copper pipes, anything. No dog's gonna keep them out."

Their talk turned to how the Mud Flats were getting worse every day, with crack vials on the playground and gunshots in the night.

Katie wished she could be alone with Mom. She wanted to say how that dog was troubling her, and then Mom would make her feel better.

She studied Jim Grady while they were busy talking. He had a scar that ran right through his eyebrow and cut it in half. There were hollows under his cheekbones. He didn't smile much, hardly ever. He had a hard face that turned soft around the eyes when he said "Mary Ann." He said "ain't." Mom always told her you had to talk right if you expected to get anyplace. Why was she with a man who said "ain't"?

Mom put the ice cream container on the table and looked at Katie. "Butter pecan!"

That was Katie's favorite kind. She loved ice cream, especially the melty part that got left on her dish. She liked to lick it off with her tongue. Mom would laugh and say "my little pussycat." Katie couldn't do that in front of Jim Grady. It was like having company in the house. Company that never went home.

CHAPTER TWO

The next day, Katie's boots squished in puddles as she hurried home from school. Sheets of rain pounded the sidewalk. The wind blew her umbrella inside out. But she went the St. Francis Street way, past the junkyard, just to see. The dog was in the back, shivering. Rain dripped from his body.

The storm continued through Saturday. Katie thought about the dog. She hoped Mr. Farrow would come to the yard and take care of him.

It was raining hard, so Katie had to stay indoors. It was awful. Mom kept saying, "Sssh, quiet. You'll wake Jim."

Jim Grady had a second job. On Friday and Saturday nights, he was a night watchman downtown.

On Sunday the weather cleared and Crystal came over. They sat on the living room floor and looked through Mom's *Vogue* magazines.

At first, they mostly whispered. "Some of those models are only fourteen years old," Crystal said.

Katie flipped through the pages. Only three years older than her? They couldn't be. They wore sheer dresses that showed *everything*..."No way!"

"Damita said."

Damita was new in school. She sat next to Crystal.

"They can't be *fourteen!*"

"They are, 'cause Damita read it. Damita says they're fixed up, that's all."

"What does she mean, fixed up?"

Crystal shrugged. "Oh, like makeup and hair and diets. Damita says they get made over."

"Linda Evangelista's not fourteen!"

"I don't know."

"She's not! Cindy Crawford's not fourteen!"

"Well, *some* of them are. A lot of them. Damita said. It was in the newspaper."

"Do you *like* Damita?"

"She's all right."

Katie watched Crystal studying the pages. Crystal had her mouth partway open, the way she did when she was concentrating. They'd been best friends forever and ever, and all of a sudden, just for a second, Crystal looked older, a pretty almost-teenager. Had her eyelashes always been that long, throwing shadows on her cheeks? When had her long blond hair formed into those soft curls?

Katie didn't have to look in the mirror to know *she* hadn't changed like that. Her hair was the same stringy, no-color light brown. She was growing fast, adding inches but just getting skinnier, with long arms and legs that got in her way.

Katie pulled the magazine onto her lap and flipped through. "They look weird. They look stupid. Look at that stupid hairdo."

She took her ballpoint and drew a mustache on one of the pouting, sexy faces. Then she added a beard. Crystal put a mustache curling way up on another one's cheeks. One of the models was smiling with her mouth wide open, so Katie drew vomit coming out of it. That's when she and Crystal started laughing out loud.

"Quiet!" Jim Grady yelled through the wall.

Katie hoped he wouldn't come out. She'd die if he started yelling at her friend! She and Crystal looked at each other.

"Sorry, girls," Mom said. "He's awful tired. Why don't you go on outside? Or to Crystal's?"

Katie didn't want to. Crystal's two little brothers would keep bothering them.

"We want to stay here," Katie said. "We'll be quiet."

"No, it's too hard for you."

So they went outside and sat on the wall in front of the building. She felt the cold of the stone through her jeans.

"Does he always yell at you?" Crystal asked.

"No, I guess not. But I wish he lived someplace else."

"But they're *married*."

"Well, I wish they weren't."

"You said you liked the wedding."

"I liked my new *dress,* that's all. Anyway, I didn't know how it would be."

Once, before the wedding, Jim took Mom and Katie to the RKO at Palmer Square, the big old movie house left over from long ago. Katie loved the ladies' room; it looked as though it belonged in a palace. And one Sunday he came to their church, fidgety in a suit, and Mom proudly introduced him to everybody. He didn't take part in any of the singing, and he never came to church with them again. But, that one time, he took them to Dorman's afterward and Katie had waffles with a pat of real butter, along with vanilla ice cream on top and a side of bacon; he'd said it was okay to order the extras. Jim and Mom did most of the talking, and it seemed all right. Katie didn't know how awful it would be to have him around every day.

"Is he mean all the time?" Crystal asked. "Is he mean to you?"

"No. Not *mean,* but—"

"So that's okay. Now you have a dad."

"Jim Grady's not my *dad!* A dad is your own *family.*"

"I guess," Crystal said. "Like at my house."

Katie's real father was no dad, either. Mom said he'd been nice but too young, that's all. But Katie couldn't help wondering how he could be nice and still leave when she was just a new little baby. Mom said she had his big brown eyes. She couldn't help wondering why he wasn't even curious to see how she was growing up. Not that it mattered. Lots of men left; all you had to do was look around the projects to see that. She didn't miss him or anything.

"It was fine when it was just me and Mom," Katie said. "We don't need anybody."

"I'd miss my dad something terrible," Crystal said.

An at-home father meant money to live in a regular apartment building; Crystal wasn't a project kid. In the projects, men came and went. "Sweet-talkin' travelin' men" was what their next-door neighbor called them. Her children all had different fathers, and none of them stuck around, not even that nice Mr. Jefferson, who used to give out lollipops. After he got laid off, Mr. Jefferson started drinking, and Katie could hear them fighting on the other side of the apartment wall. Then he left and everything quieted down over there.

Mom was smart; she had stayed on her own. She'd finished high school at night, and now she had a job at the hospital downtown—it was an important one, too, because she checked people's insurance and stuff when they came in—so they'd been off welfare for a long time. Katie caught her breath; what if Jim Grady made a new baby and took off? They'd be right back where they started!

"My daddy's so funny," Crystal was saying.

"The way he carries on, imitating people's voices. He can make me laugh so hard I have to pee!"

"My mom makes me laugh," Katie said.

They threw a ball against the brick wall until they got tired of it. They watched some teenage girls jumping double Dutch. Then Katie walked Crystal partway home. They stopped at the junkyard. The junkyard dog was licking and licking at an empty tin pan.

"Look, he's thirsty," Katie said. "Mr. Farrow's not taking care of him."

"He doesn't come to the junkyard much," Crystal said. "That's why he got a guard dog."

"But he doesn't even have water to drink!"

"Oh, well..." Crystal shrugged. "See you in school tomorrow."

She continued home and Katie stayed at the fence. The dog had given up on the tin pan. He lay on the ground next to a pile of rusty things. His tongue was hanging out.

Katie ran home and filled an empty milk container with water. Mom wasn't in the kitchen, so Katie took a saucer from the sink and tiptoed out. She poured the water into the saucer when she got back to the fence. She could just manage to slip it underneath.

"Here," she said.

He didn't move. He stood way back, with his tail between his legs.

"Come on. Here's a drink."

The dog took one tentative step. He sniffed at the air.

"Listen, I've got to take that plate back home, so if you want this water, you better have it right now."

He wouldn't come any closer. Katie moved away from the fence and waited.

Finally, thirst got the best of him. He came over and lapped up the water quickly, every last drop. Then he backed off, though not quite as far.

"Good dog," Katie said.

She was surprised by his instant reaction to those words. He raised his head and pricked up his ears. He seemed to look hopeful.

"Good dog," she repeated.

His tail hesitantly began to wag.

Katie refilled the saucer and he came right up next to her. His tongue made sloshing noises as he drank eagerly. Boy, she'd never seen anyone *that* thirsty!

When he finished, he stayed at the fence. Katie was crouched down; they were eye to eye.

"Good dog," she whispered.

He poked the tip of his nose against the links.

"I bet no one ever pets you," she said. Her hand wouldn't fit through. "But I can't reach you."

They looked into each other's eyes for the longest time.

"I'll be back," she promised.

CHAPTER THREE

Jim Grady nodded as he bit into the drumstick. "It's good."

"That's honey-pepper coating." Mom beamed. "My Aunt Geraldine's recipe."

All he'd said was that one word and Mom's face was all lit up. "Good." Big deal.

"I know about a million different ways to make chicken," Mom said.

"You don't need to go to all that trouble—"

"But I *want* to, hon." Mom leaned over him and ruffled his hair, and Jim pulled her down onto his knee.

Katie didn't want to look at them. She got busy putting things on her plate—rice and broccoli, and then she picked through until she found a piece of white-meat chicken breast.

Mostly Mom used to be too tired to cook when she came home from work. They'd take TV dinners out of the freezer. But ever since Jim Grady came, it was like Sunday dinner every night of the week. That was the only good part about having him around.

Maybe Mom was turning herself inside out for him so he wouldn't go. Well, it would be a relief if he did.

They were talking about money things. Jim was saying, "...enough for a down payment..." Katie wasn't interested. She wondered if Mr. Farrow had come to give the junkyard dog some dinner. He was so skinny. He must be starved.

A dog would like chicken, she knew that for sure. Maybe rice and broccoli would be good for him, too. But mostly chicken...

Katie carefully spread her napkin on her lap. Mom and Jim were too busy with each other to notice anything. She slipped some broccoli off her plate and into the napkin.

It was already dark; Mom wouldn't let her go out by herself after dinner. But she'd stop at the junkyard on the way to school in the morning. Katie slid the chicken from her plate. It would be a big treat!

She didn't want to get her jeans greasy. She adjusted the napkin and...

"What are you doing under there, Katie?" Mom said. At the very same moment, the piece of chicken fell on the floor.

Mom and Jim stared at the broccoli in her napkin, and at the chicken next to her foot. Then they both stared at her.

"What is this?" Jim said. "Don't take it if you don't want it, but you're not throwing out good food!"

He wasn't exactly yelling. But his voice was so deep, it sounded like yelling. Katie felt her face getting hot.

Mom looked puzzled. "You *like* fried chicken..."

Jim looked mad. "I work hard to put something on the table!"

"I wasn't going to throw it out," Katie said. "Mom, I was saving it for the dog, that's all. You should see how hungry he is!"

"What dog?" Mom said.

"The *junkyard* dog! Farrow's junkyard. Mr. Farrow doesn't come to take care of him or anything, and he was thirsty and...You should have seen the way he drank up the water I gave him. Like he'd never have enough!"

"Oh, no," Mom said. "Stay away from there. I don't want you playing with junkyard dogs!"

"But—"

"He could be vicious. What if he bites? No, Katie, I won't allow—"

"He won't bite me."

"No, it's dangerous." Mom looked upset. She wouldn't listen. Well, at least *he* wasn't butting in.

Katie took a deep breath. "Mom, he's much too skinny. And he has the saddest eyes. And he's getting to like me. And I promised—"

"I don't want you hanging around the junkyard," Mom said. "And I don't want to hear another word about it."

Katie bit her lip. She'd been sure Mom would understand. Maybe if Jim Grady hadn't been there, getting mad… She watched miserably as Mom picked up the chicken from the floor and headed toward the garbage pail.

"Wait a minute, Mary Ann," Jim said.

Mom turned to him.

"White-meat chicken's pretty luxurious dog food"—Jim's lips twisted into a half-smile—"but it's no good to us anymore, is it? So why not—"

"That's not the point." Mom looked annoyed. "He could attack Katie! You can't tell what a junkyard dog might do."

"Well," he said, "why don't Katie and I take a walk over there after dinner? I'll check him out. I know dogs, Mary Ann."

Mom sighed. "I don't know…"

"Please, please," Katie said. "I've *got* to feed him!"

Mom hesitated. "Okay, but don't let her get too close."

"He's fenced in," Katie said. "I can't even reach in to *pet* him."

"Well, that's good," Mom said. "Don't touch him."

Katie wrapped up the chicken and broccoli in her napkin. She couldn't wait to see how happy the dog would be. But what if he growled at Jim Grady? He might. What if Jim Grady told Mom he was just a mean old junkyard dog?

CHAPTER FOUR

The project playground was deserted and the swings looked strange and shadowy in the dark. Jim Grady walked with giant steps, and Katie had to go double-time to keep up.

They turned the corner and went by the gas station. Katie tried to hold her breath until they were past it. She got a noseful of fumes anyway.

There wasn't a sound except for their footsteps. She tried to think of something to say to him. There was still a way to go before they reached the junkyard. Maybe she should tell him to come up to the fence real slow, so he wouldn't scare the dog. Maybe she'd better not. Sometimes grown-ups didn't like being told what to do, especially by a kid.

Katie could hear a car alarm wailing over on the avenue. It kept going and going. Hardly anyone was out on the sidewalk. Trouble happened after dark.

She glanced up at Jim Grady. He walked along like he owned St. Francis Street. He was so big. No one would mess with him, that was for sure. Even after they passed the streetlamp's circle of light, she felt safe next to him. Safe, but he had her half-running. His legs were too long!

"Make sure you take the bones off the chicken," he said.

"Dogs love bones," Katie answered.

"Real thick bones, like a shank bone, are okay," he said. "Little bones break up; they can choke a dog."

"All right," she gasped.

He noticed. "What's the matter with you?" he asked.

"You're walking too fast for me."

"Sorry, I guess I'm not used to kids." He slowed down to a stroll. "Listen, when I forget you're just a little girl, you let me know."

"I'm not little. I'm eleven!"

"Right."

Even before they reached the junkyard, Katie could hear the dog barking. They were drawn-out barks that ended on a high pitch. She was worried. What would Jim think?

"He doesn't bark all the time," she said quickly. "Hardly ever."

"Sounds like pure loneliness to me," Jim said.

They came to the chain-link fence. The links glistened in the street light. She couldn't see the dog; he had to be in the dark in the back of the yard. He was quiet now. She could feel him watching and listening.

"Don't feed him yet," Jim said. "Let me check him out."

Jim crouched down next to the fence. "Here boy, come here."

The dog moved out of the shadows. He stood away from them, stiff-legged and on guard. He sniffed the air suspiciously. Katie heard a low growl. Please be nice, she prayed silently.

Standing stock-still and surrounded by shadows, the dog looked scary. Katie was glad she wasn't all alone.

"Here, dog," she called. "It's me."

At the sound of her voice, the dog's body relaxed. He came right to the fence. His tail was wagging. He recognized her from yesterday! She didn't know he'd remember her. She'd really made friends with him!

Jim put his hand flat against the fence and let the dog sniff it for a while.

"See, he's nice," Katie said. "Isn't he?"

Jim stayed crouched down. "Sit," he commanded.

The dog hesitated for a second. Then, very slowly, he sat.

"Down," Jim said.

The dog lowered his front paws and head to the ground. He kept his eyes on Jim.

Katie was amazed by the way the dog understood the words. That proved he was smart. Jim could tell Mom he was smart *and* nice.

"Okay, good dog," Jim said, and the dog bounded up, his tail wagging a mile a minute. He looked at Jim expectantly.

"Good dog," Jim repeated. "You want a good scratching behind your ears, don't you boy? Sorry I can't reach you. Good dog."

"You like him, right?" Katie asked.

"He was trained. He was somebody's pet," Jim said. "He must have been lost or abandoned."

"How do you know all that?" Katie asked.

"This dog trusted people once, and not that long ago, either. Look at him. He's ready to trust again if he gets half a chance." Jim sighed. "Well, he's in for a real hard time. The way a dog's mind works, he thinks it's his fault when he's being mistreated."

Katie felt something squeezing her heart. Jim wasn't used to talking to kids, that was for sure; he just went right ahead and made her feel terrible.

"Okay, give him his food."

She pulled off the chicken and wrapped the bones in the napkin. Then she slid the meat and broccoli under the fence. They watched the dog wolfing everything down. She couldn't believe how fast he swallowed.

"He must've been awful hungry to eat the broccoli," Jim said. "Anybody that would voluntarily eat *broccoli*..."

"I *like* broccoli," Katie said. "It's my most favorite vegetable." She looked at him suspiciously. "You ate it at dinner."

"Wouldn't want to hurt your mama's feelings."

Katie sat down cross-legged next to the fence. The dog wriggled against it, as close to her as he could get. She wished she could touch him. "You're gonna tell Mom it's okay to feed him, right?"

"I guess. Only it's not gonna be chicken off our table. Buy him some dog food if you want."

"Okay, I'll ask Mom to—"

"No way. You get an allowance, don't you? If you're gonna feed him, it's on you."

Her allowance! Her allowance was for candy and magazines and...Katie bit her lip and nodded.

Jim was looking at her sideways. He stood up and reached into his pocket. "Here's a dollar to get you started, but that's all. Don't be asking me or Mary Ann; there's none to spare."

"I bet Mom would *love* him. Look how beautiful his eyes are."

"Don't bet on it. Mary Ann's not used to animals 'cause she's been in the projects all her life. Now me, I grew up in the country. I had a hound dog name of Rex that followed me everyplace..."

Katie squeezed her fingers under the fence. The dog licked the tips. His tongue felt wet and sandpapery. "I'm calling him Lucky," she said, "'cause his luck is gonna change."

Jim shook his head. "Don't name him. He's not your dog and he's not about to be."

A raggedy old man pushing an overloaded shopping cart passed by. The wheels scraped and squeaked against the pavement.

Far off, a siren cut through the night.

"Come on," Jim said. "Time to go home."

Katie got up reluctantly. The dog was pressed against the fence. As she moved away to follow Jim, she thought she heard a soft whimper. She turned; the dog's eyes were still on her. Every couple of steps, she looked back over her shoulder. Even when she couldn't see Lucky anymore, she *knew* he was still at the fence, his eyes still on the spot where she'd gone, waiting and hoping.

"I'll ask Mr. Farrow," Katie said. "I'll ask if I can have him." Mr. Farrow looked mean and scruffy; she'd have to be brave to talk to him.

"You know there's no pets allowed in the projects."

"But what if nobody finds out? If he's quiet— he'll be very quiet and—"

"No way. We're not getting evicted over a dog. You know the waiting list?"

"But what if—I'd take such good care of him, I would, and—"

"Forget it, Katie. There's no way."

"There *has* to be a way. My teacher says if you want something bad enough…"

"I'm the first to believe in goals—hell, I'm working two jobs toward a goal—but you better learn the difference between what's possible and what ain't."

"My teacher says faith can move mountains."

"Maybe I ought to set her straight. She ought to be teaching you to pick your way around obstacles instead of telling you to wish them away."

Katie glared at Jim. Everybody knew Mrs. Ryan was the best teacher in the whole school.

"I can't leave Lucky in the junkyard!"

"Even if you could take that dog in—and you can't—Farrow would get himself another one in a minute. So then another dog would be in the exact same spot. What good would that do?"

This was the most talking Katie had ever done with Jim Grady. And she didn't like the things he was saying.

Maybe she could hide Lucky... Where, in the broom closet? Maybe she could... She'd think of something.

Just before they went through the door of the building, Katie looked up at the sky. Way up high, above the roof across the street, there was a sliver of moon and a sprinkling of stars.

"Star light, star bright, first star I see tonight..." she whispered to herself. Somehow, some way, she would rescue Lucky!

CHAPTER FIVE

"I don't like it," Mom said. "He could be diseased or—"

"Come on, Mary Ann. She's not touching him. She's not gonna catch anything from putting food down."

"It's Farrow's dog. It's not her responsibility."

"Yeah, but she likes him."

"I *love* him!" Katie said.

"He's a nice enough animal and it's true, he's half-starved." Jim put his arm around Mom's shoulders. "Come on, babe, let her; there's no harm in it."

"Well...I don't know," she said slowly. "If you

really think it's all right... Now listen to me, Katie. You wash your hands every time. As soon as you leave him. With lots of soap and hot water, you hear me?"

"I promise," Katie said. She usually didn't like the way Jim Grady could sweet-talk Mom into just about anything, but this one time she was glad.

Mom rummaged in the bottom of the cabinet and pulled out an old tinfoil pan. "Here. I guess you can have this for his water."

"Thanks!" Katie gave her a bear hug. "Thanks, thanks, thanks!"

Boy, Mom would be so mad if she knew about her blue-and-white china saucer that first time! But Katie had scrubbed it out good afterward, she really had...

The next day, Katie left school with Crystal and Meg. They automatically walked down the street to Carter's, the newspaper and candy store in the middle of the block. At three o'clock the narrow aisle was jammed with kids.

They worked their way through the crowd. Crystal frowned at the candy display. She picked up a Milky Way and then put it down again.

"Hey! No touching if you're not buying," Mr. Carter said.

"I'm *deciding!*" Crystal said.

"You kids," he grumbled.

"A Mars Bar or a Milky Way. I don't know. What are you getting?"

"Almond Joy," Meg said. "I like nuts." She handed over her money.

"*You're* a nut!" Crystal laughed. "What about you, Katie? Want to get a Mars *and* a Milky Way, and share?"

"I'm not getting anything," Katie mumbled.

"You're not?"

Katie had to turn away; she could smell the chocolate right through the paper wrapping. It made her mouth water.

Daniel, Eddie, John, and Leroy, the worst boys in her class, came rushing in, pushing past everybody. They were horsing around making noise. All of a sudden, Meg started giggling nervously. She was acting so dumb! Katie raised her eyebrows; she was about to exchange glances with Crystal, but Crystal was looking at the boys, too, and flipping her hair over her shoulder. Katie didn't care that much about Meg, but was *Crystal* getting boy-crazy? It gave her a prickly, all-alone feeling, as if everybody was jumping aboard a train and she was left behind at the station.

The boys ignored them, but Crystal and Meg were staying in the store extra time for no good reason. They'd already paid for their candy, hadn't they?

Other kids were shoving on their way to the counter.

"Come on, let's go," Katie said.

Outside, Meg sighed. "Daniel's hot."

"Damita says he's *blazing*," Crystal added.

Were they crazy? Daniel was the worst of all of them. He was always yelling things out in class, and Mrs. Ryan had to keep telling him to settle down.

Crystal carefully unwrapped her candy bar. "How come you didn't get anything? Want a bite?"

"Well…just a little one." Katie took a baby bite. It was all she could do not to chomp off a huge mouthful.

"Don't you have any money?" Meg asked.

"Katie gets an allowance," Crystal said. "Every single Friday, right?"

"I'm saving it. I have to buy something."

"What?"

"Dog food."

Crystal stared. "You don't have a dog."

"Hey, did you get a puppy?" Meg got excited. "Let's go see it!"

"No," Katie said. "It's for the junkyard dog."

"How come?" Crystal asked. "What do you want to feed him for?"

"I just do...My mom said I could. I'm gonna go feed him every day before dinner, before it gets dark."

"Gee," Crystal said. "Do you have to pay for it out of your allowance?"

"Sort of. Well, Jim Grady gave me a dollar."

"That's all he gave you? I bet dog food's more than that."

"I don't know. I'll see at the store."

"That Jim Grady sure is stingy," Crystal said.

Katie stiffened. "No, he's not." It wasn't right for someone outside the family to say things about him. Even if it was true. "He said there's nothing to spare."

"Oh, sure," Crystal said. "Your mom works, and he works *two* jobs! You said. Carpenter and night watchman. He's making plenty. He's just plain stingy."

"He is not!"

"What are you getting mad about? You don't like him."

"No," Katie said. "Well, he's not that bad."

"He's not nice. Remember how he yelled at us?"

"Just that one time, because he needed his sleep!" There was an edge to Katie's voice. "He doesn't yell all the time!"

"Now *you're* yelling."

"Oh. I didn't mean to."

Crystal looked down. "Okay, I don't care," she mumbled. "I was just saying what you said yourself."

Crystal was right. And tiptoeing around all day Saturday and Sunday while Jim was sleeping was a real pain.

"Well, what do you want to do?" Crystal asked.

"Let's wait for the boys to come out," Meg said, "and see where they go."

"You mean *follow* them?" Katie asked.

"We could just hang around and..." Crystal twirled her hair around her finger.

"I'm going to the store," Katie said. "I want to get dinner for the dog." She was worried about how much dog food would cost. "Want to come?"

Crystal shook her head. "Why are you fooling around with that junkyard dog, anyway?"

"You could get a cute little puppy," Meg said.

"You could get a cute puppy at the shelter."

"I don't want a puppy!"

"Well, excu-use me," Meg said.

"Katie?" Crystal said. "You can have another bite."

"No thanks. Thanks anyway, I mean it." She swallowed. She had to keep her mind off the melty-soft, dark, sweet chocolate covering chewy caramel...

"So...I'm staying around here, okay?" Crystal said. "See you tomorrow."

"Okay, see you."

Katie had gone a few steps when Crystal called after her.

"Watch out for Farrow! You better make sure he doesn't catch you!"

Katie sighed. She didn't want to think about that at all.

At the Associated, she studied the big bags of dry dog food. First she reached up and took the cheapest one. But then she thought maybe it wouldn't be good enough, so she stood on her toes to put it back on the shelf.

There were so many kinds. She wished Crystal and Meg had come to help her choose. Finally, she picked the one she'd seen on that TV commercial. It had a man with a whole bunch of prize-winning purebred dogs, and they were running in the grass. He said that was the only brand for *his* dogs. Well, Lucky deserved just as good as those purebreds. She wished he could be happy and playing in the grass, too.

At the checkout counter, Katie handed over Jim's dollar and most of her allowance. She tried not to feel bad when it disappeared into the cash register.

CHAPTER SIX

Even though Damita was brand-new in school, she was going to be Pocahontas in the Thanksgiving play and Katie only got to be in the crowd of Pilgrims! The truth was, at tryouts Damita's voice was the loudest; she didn't seem a bit embarrassed about acting in front of the whole class. Crystal and Meg were just regular Indians. Daniel was the leader of the Pilgrims, and he knew his lines pretty well. But when other people were rehearsing, he kept fooling around with Leroy. Mrs. Ryan had to keep telling them to keep quiet and sit down. Boys were troublemakers, that's all.

"So here's some corn and turkey and pumpkin

pie for you," Damita/Pocahontas was saying.

Pumpkin pie. Way back when Katie was little, Mom had bought one for Thanksgiving at the day-old bakery outlet. It looked so good, all orange and creamy, that Katie couldn't *wait*. She had to eat her vegetables first, and then...but it didn't taste anything like she expected! It had a funny taste that made Katie spit it out on the first bite. Mom threw the whole pie away and started to cry. "I bought spoiled pie," she said, sobbing and gulping. "Spoiled pie for my baby!" She was crying so hard, with tears running in a stream down her cheeks, as if she wouldn't ever stop, and Katie was scared. That was a long time ago. They didn't have to buy at the day-old place anymore, but Katie still didn't like pumpkin pie.

"Make sure you get your costumes made in time for dress rehearsal," Mrs. Ryan said. She gave out patterns, crepe paper, and cardboard.

Every day after school, Katie and Crystal worked on their costumes. Seemed that they did everything at Crystal's house because there was no room for anything at Katie's anymore.

And on Thursday afternoons, Katie had P.A.L. basketball in the school gym. That was the one place where being tall for her age didn't feel awkward and everything about her body worked.

She wouldn't miss basketball practice for anything! But no matter how busy she was, she stopped at the junkyard before dinnertime to feed Lucky and keep him company. It was hard to take care of someone and have him count on her. She didn't always feel like going out in the cold again after she got home. Once, she skipped a day and then she felt guilty all night; she knew Lucky had waited for her, hungry and hoping. She never skipped a day again, except when Mr. Farrow was there. Even from a distance, there was a real mean look on his face, like he was mad at the whole world. His cracked brown leather jacket barely covered his stocky body and the waist of his pants hung down below his stomach as he stomped around. When Katie saw Mr. Farrow in the yard, she went on by.

Spending time with Lucky meant that she had to do her homework after dinner. By the time she finished her homework, it was sometimes too late for her favorite TV shows. That would have been all right—it was worth it for Lucky. He came running to her now, just like her very own dog! But sometimes she missed her best shows even when her homework was done. All because of Jim Grady. He had to watch his own dumb show just when *Full House* was on! And he always held the remote in his hand and kept switching channels whenever *he* wanted to.

"How come he gets to hog the TV?" she asked Mom when they were alone.

"Katie, he works hard and needs to relax."

"Well, it's *our* television!"

"Oh, no. We're a *family*. Everything here is everybody's."

"I never get to see *Full House!*"

"Maybe the two of you could take turns…"

"No matter what's on, he keeps switching channels! He keeps doing that!"

Mom laughed. "I know, men are like that."

Katie didn't think it was funny. If men had to be like that, it was better not to have one hanging around.

There were some good parts to having Jim Grady there, though. A man in the house made Mom feel better. Before he came, she used to double-check the locks on the door before they went to bed, even though she *knew* she had locked them. She didn't do that now. And she smiled a lot and looked prettier than ever and even sang as she did stuff around the house.

But for Katie, that didn't make up for not getting the TV, or being so crowded, or having to whisper and tiptoe all day Saturday and

Sunday when he was sleeping.

One Sunday Katie was talking to Mom when Jim Grady woke up and came into the living room.

"Lucky knows me really well now," Katie was saying. "You should see the way his tail wags when I come."

"Mmm-hmm." Mom turned a shirt around on the ironing board.

"He gobbles up everything I give him, he likes it so much, and you can tell he's thankful. He always looks up at me first, just before he starts eating, and his eyes are so—"

"Uh-huh."

Katie could tell that she was listening with only half an ear. She wished Mom was more interested. She was bursting to tell somebody about how sweet Lucky was and how much she loved him.

"That dog's looking better," Jim said.

"I feed him every day except when Mr. Farrow's around."

"I passed by the other day; I could see he's filling out."

Even Jim Grady had noticed. That meant she was making a real difference for Lucky!

• • • • •

The next day after school, Katie rushed to the junkyard. It was getting dark earlier these days. The streetlamp wasn't on yet, but the daylight was turning into a gray haze.

Lucky was waiting at the fence. He was so smart; he knew she'd be coming.

"Hi, Lucky!"

The dog's body wriggled with anticipation.

"Guess what I have for you! Last night's leftover meatloaf!" That would be a special treat after all that dry dog food. She reached into her bag. "Jim Grady said I could—"

"Hey, you!"

Mr. Farrow! He was coming from the back of the yard! Katie was too scared to move.

"You the one's been feeding my dog?" He was at the fence, yelling right into her face. He was unshaven. His pale, puffy skin was spotted with brown liver marks.

"Uh-huh," she said. She could hardly talk.

"You stay away, you hear me?"

There was a low growl from Lucky.

"Shut up, mutt!" Mr. Farrow raised his arm and Lucky cringed.

"He...he's hungry." Her voice came out in a squeak. "I was only feeding him, that's all."

"He's *my* damn dog; I *want* him hungry and

mean! Now get outta here! Git!"

Katie ran, with the meatloaf still in the bag. She knew Lucky had smelled it and now… She almost started to cry. Lucky had to be so disappointed, and the way that man was yelling at her… She ran all the way home, her heart pounding.

"What happened to you?" Jim Grady was sitting in the kitchen. He must have just come in; he was unlacing his boots.

Katie told him about Mr. Farrow, but she didn't let her eyes get teary in front of him.

"Well, that's a problem." Jim frowned. "It *is* his dog."

"I can't let Lucky down! He's expecting—"

"Mmmm." Jim pulled off the first boot. "You're gonna have to get his permission."

"Mr. Farrow's permission?"

"You have to talk to him."

"But how?" Katie asked. "I can't!"

"Find something to say that'll change his mind."

Katie bit her lip. "I could say…I could say he doesn't feed Lucky enough or take care of him and it's so cruel…and I could say Lucky's such a nice dog, and…" Her voice trailed off. She couldn't imagine talking to Mr. Farrow.

"That won't do it. He doesn't care about that. You got to offer him something he wants."

"Something he wants?"

"Something that's in his interest. Okay, what does he want Lucky for?"

"To guard the junkyard."

Jim grunted as he pulled off the other boot. "What do you think a good guard dog should be like?"

First she was going to say "mean," but that wouldn't help anything. She thought for a while. "Big and strong?"

Jim nodded.

"He needs food to be strong?"

"The dog's got to be healthy if he's gonna guard anything. If he's starved, he's gonna lie in a corner and fade away. Or take meat from any thief that comes along."

"Will Mr. Farrow listen?"

"I don't know." Jim stretched out his legs. "You can hit him in his pocket, too. If *you're* feeding the dog, that don't cost him a cent."

Katie started feeling hopeful.

"The truth is, a dog naturally guards his own territory," Jim said. "Keeping him miserable won't make him any better. But a lowlife like Farrow can't see that."

"Would you go talk to him right now?" Katie asked. "So Lucky can have his meatloaf?"

"Not me," Jim said. "You, Katie."

"Me?"

"If you want permission, go ask for it." He got up and took a can of beer out of the refrigerator.

"I can't!"

Jim shrugged. "That's up to you."

"Please?" Katie said. "Please do it for me?"

"You'll never get what you want if you don't learn to ask for it. Even from a grown-up." He sat down again, popped the can, took a long swallow, and wiped his mouth with his hand.

"He'll yell at me!"

"Maybe he'll listen to you, maybe he won't. You won't know until you try."

Katie glared at Jim. If Mom was home, she'd never make me do this all by myself, Katie thought. I'm only a kid. He doesn't understand anything!

"Mr. Farrow's mean," Katie said, "and rough."

Jim nodded. "I know."

He isn't moving, Katie thought. He really isn't going to take care of it for me.

But she had to try, for Lucky. Right now,

before it got dark, while Mr. Farrow was still there. A big lump came into her throat.

She walked out the door, clutching the bag. She walked stiffly because she was so scared. And she hated Jim Grady!

CHAPTER SEVEN

Again Katie carried the meatloaf in its brown paper bag to the junkyard. She dragged her feet as she walked along the sidewalk. Twice she almost turned around and went back home. But what would become of Lucky if she couldn't feed him anymore?

Mr. Farrow was making a pile of some metal pipes in the junkyard and didn't notice her coming toward the fence. But Lucky did. He moved toward her slowly, not running and jumping the way he usually did. Lucky kept an eye on Mr. Farrow; he knew there might be trouble.

Katie took a deep breath. "Mr. Farrow?" He didn't even hear her. She tried again. "Mr. Farrow?"

The man looked up. "You again?" he snarled. "Didn't I tell you to stay away?"

"I need to tell…um…ask you something."

"Get outta here. I'm busy!"

Katie stood still, looking at him. She didn't know what to say.

Farrow smashed a pipe on the pile; it clanged loudly. He stalked to the fence. Lucky stiffened. Katie wanted to run away, but she made herself stay.

"All right! What d'you want?" He was yelling right into her face.

She flinched.

"Cat got your tongue, girl?"

"Uh, you want a good guard dog and…if a burglar came and—" Katie was so scared that the words came out jumbled.

Farrow stared at her. "What?" His eyes were yellow where they were supposed to be white.

With the sun gone, it was very cold. Katie shivered. Her lips felt stiff as she spoke. "If the dog gets too thin, he won't be strong enough to… You want him strong, right?"

Farrow shrugged. "So long's he can bark."

"If he's real hungry, somebody could just give him a piece of meat and get in your yard."

He snorted a laugh. "If the mutt's real hungry,

he'll take a bite outta somebody's leg."

Katie tried to think of something to say. She took another deep breath. "A skinny dog doesn't scare anybody away."

"I throw him something when I come around," Farrow said.

"He needs food and water every day," Katie said.

"The more he eats, the more he messes."

"That's not his fault!" How could anyone be so stupid and mean?

"Quit bothering me," Farrow said. "I have work to do."

"He'd be a lot better watchdog," Katie said quickly. "Jim Grady said so and he knows about dogs. No one could trick him with a bone or something. It's less trouble for you if I feed him."

Farrow waved her away and started toward the back.

"Mr. Farrow!" Katie called. "I'll buy his food. It won't cost you anything. Not a penny."

Farrow turned around. "You want to pay for it?"

Katie nodded quickly.

He stared at her like she was crazy. Then he shrugged. "So go ahead, no skin off my back."

That had to mean permission, Katie thought.

She held her breath. That meant permission!

Farrow moved away and went back to working with the metal pipes.

"It's okay, Lucky," Katie said softly. "I did it!"

Lucky acted different with Mr. Farrow close by. He was cautious, his tail down. It made her think that maybe Mr. Farrow beat him. A crawly feeling went up her back.

She slipped the meatloaf under the fence. Lucky wolfed it down. She could tell he loved it. His tongue darted out again and again, licking the last bits from his mouth.

"Don't worry, I'll take care of you," she whispered. "You're a good dog and I love you."

Lucky's tail slowly began to wag.

Every once in a while, Farrow glanced at them.

"I can't stay today," Katie whispered. "Not with him around. But I did it! I got permission!"

Katie skipped down the hall to the apartment. She couldn't wait to tell Jim Grady!

Even before she unlocked the door, she could hear that Mom had come home from work. Mom sounded really mad.

"How could you send her there by herself?" Mom was saying. "She's only a little girl and—"

"Wait a minute, I didn't *send* her," Jim said. "I left it up to her."

"Well, you shouldn't have! You had no business—"

"I'm sorry, but—maybe it's not my place to say this—but you're babying her too much, Mary Ann."

"You don't know the first thing about children!"

"It's good for her to take care of things for herself."

"She doesn't have to!" Mom sounded furious. "I don't want her to! That awful man could—"

"He's not gonna hurt her, all he'll do is yell and—"

Katie burst into the living room. "It's okay!" she sang out. "I talked to him. I didn't even care about his yelling. I got permission!"

"Oh, Katie," Mom said. "If I'd been home—"

"Now I can feed Lucky forever and ever." Katie couldn't stop smiling. "I got permission all by myself. I hit him right in the pocket, just like you said."

"Even so—" Mom started.

"Look at her," Jim said. "She's feeling pretty good about herself."

Katie grinned at him. "Uh-huh."

"Now you know. If you want something, go ahead and ask," Jim said. "Even if it's a grown-up."

Katie looked at him. "*Any* grown-up?"

"So long as you're respectful," Mom said. "Always be respectful."

"That's right," Jim said. "Listen to your mama."

Katie's grin widened. "All right, Mister Jim Grady. I've been meaning to ask about something. It's not fair for you to always get your shows. Tonight ought to be my turn; I want to watch *Full House* after dinner."

Jim stared at her for such a long moment that Katie began to feel anxious. Then he started roaring with laughter.

"Good God, Mary Ann," he gasped, "I made a Frankenstein monster here."

Mom started to laugh, too. Katie was glad they weren't fighting anymore. It was nice, with the three of them laughing so hard.

CHAPTER EIGHT

A rusted refrigerator appeared in the junkyard. It lay on its side without a door. On rainy days, Katie would see Lucky huddled in it. It was wide open and it didn't keep all the rain out. She'd see him shake his body to throw off the water. At least he had some kind of protection, Katie thought, but she worried about him when the weather was bad.

Then the refrigerator disappeared.

One day, Katie saw Mr. Farrow in the yard. Mostly she didn't talk to him, but this time she said, "Where's that refrigerator? Lucky needs it."

"Who's lucky?" Farrow snorted. "No one's lucky around here."

"But where's the refrigerator?"

"Sold it off," he said.

There was no shelter for Lucky at all, just when he needed it most.

It was a cold December. Katie wore an extra sweater under her parka. It made her arms feel so stiff that she could hardly bend her elbows. And Mom made her wear the dumb cap that Grandma Hattie had knitted.

"I don't need to wear *that*," she complained.

"Yes you do," Mom said. "You've got to have something on your head."

"No I don't!"

"Stop sassing your mama," Jim Grady said. Why did he have to butt in?

"Can I at least get a new hat? This has *rabbits* on it! Just because Grandma made it—"

"I know." Mom looked sympathetic. "Maybe we'll go shopping and—"

Jim Grady interrupted. "There's no need to go out buying new things when that cap ain't even worn out yet."

Katie didn't say anything, but she thought Crystal was right about him. He was plain stingy.

"He won't let my mom buy me a new hat," she told Crystal when they met outside the school. Her ears were freezing because she'd pulled the cap off and stuck it in her pocket as soon as she'd left home.

"Maybe you could cuff it." Crystal got busy folding over the bottom. "See, that almost hides the bunnies."

"They still show," Katie said. "Look at them! I just won't wear it."

"You'll need *something* when we go sledding," Crystal said.

"Say what?" Katie said. "There's no snow."

"On TV, they said snow this week," Crystal answered. "We'll go belly-whopping on Devil's Run, right? I hope it snows all winter! I asked for a saucer for Christmas 'cause they're lots faster than sleds and—"

"Maybe I'll get a saucer, too." Devil's Run was what all the kids called the steep sledding hill past the bridge, where St. Francis Street met Sycamore; it was scary and exciting!

"I sure hope it snows by..." Katie continued, and then she suddenly turned quiet. What would Lucky do in the snow?

The sleet had started that afternoon. It wasn't sticking to the sidewalk, but there were slushy patches on the wet pavement. Heavy needles of ice pelted Katie's head as she went to feed Lucky. Reluctantly, she pulled on the stupid cap. The wind whipped under her parka.

Lucky came running the minute she arrived at the fence. His fur was matted and dripping. Bits of ice were crusted on it.

"Just regular dog food today," Katie said. "Hurry up and eat before it gets all wet." She slipped the pan of water under the fence, too; drops of ice rippled its surface.

Even as he was eating, Lucky shivered. When he'd finished, Katie squeezed her fingertips through the links. As always, he licked them and pushed against the fence, trying to get closer.

"It's so cold. I've got to put my mittens back on."

He stayed close, his body trembling.

"I know, you're freezing. I don't know what to do."

She looked around the yard. No sign of Mr. Farrow. She looked at the door cut into the fence. She rattled the big, heavy lock. There was no way to open it.

"I wish I could take you home. I'd keep you nice and warm and make a special bed with a soft blanket and…"

If there were any way to get him out, she'd

take him home, even if it was against project rules. She couldn't leave him like this!

"We'll sit right next to the radiator and I'll dry you off with a big towel and I'll pet you and..." She could *see* them, curled up together in the living room, so cozy and contented, and she'd be brushing out his fur and making it shine.

He had a way of cocking his head as though he was trying hard to understand her words. His eyes never left her face.

She heard the mournful horn of a tugboat on the river.

"I wish I could." Her breath looked like smoke in the air. "I'm sorry, Lucky. I don't know what to do."

She stayed with him until her feet were numb with cold.

When she left, she kept glancing back over her shoulder. He was out in the open, shivering, his whole body pointed toward her.

That night, the man on TV said it was record cold for December. Katie sat on the couch with Mom and Jim Grady. She sipped at a cup of hot chocolate. She could feel the sweet warmth going right down to her stomach.

"With the windchill factor," the man said, "it's twenty below zero. Exposure for even a few moments can cause frostbite, so keep those gloves and ski masks on. An advisory is out for…"

The radiator hissed.

The picture on TV showed some people leading an old lady out of a big cardboard box.

"City workers are out in force tonight to convince the homeless to come into municipal shelters…."

The wind rattled the windowpanes. Katie felt the draft.

"…with urgency in seeking out the hidden or reluctant homeless. There is the very real danger of death by exposure on this coldest of December nights…."

Tears welled up in Katie's eyes.

"Honey, what is it?" Mom said.

"'Death by exposure,'" she gulped. "That means *freezing* to death!"

"Don't worry," Mom said. "They'll find all the people. They'll be all right."

"Maybe, maybe not," Jim said.

Katie saw Mom shoot him a look.

"The fact is," Jim said, "some people die on the streets every winter. I'm sorry, Mary Ann, we can't pretend that away."

"What about Lucky?" Katie wailed. "He's out in the cold all by himself!"

"Animals take care of themselves, sweetie." Mom put an arm around her shoulders. "Don't forget, they've got their fur coats."

Katie knew Mom would soft-soap things for her. She turned to Jim. "Is that true?"

"Lucky's been outdoors all along, so he's grown a winter coat. That helps some," Jim said. "He's probably hurting tonight, but he's got a chance."

"Please let me bring him home! Please! Let's go get him right now!"

"Even if we could take him out of the yard— and we can't—he can't come here," Jim said. "We talked about that. We're not getting evicted over this."

"You're getting too attached," Mom said.

"I love him!"

"He's not your dog, honey," Mom said.

"What difference does it make *whose* dog he is?" Katie cried. "He's out there, cold and…and hurting!"

"You've done a lot for him," Jim said. "Regular food gave him a layer of fat, and that'll help keep him warm….You got enough dog food?"

Katie nodded.

"Well, then, you've done the best you can."

"But even if he's okay tonight…" Katie bit her lip. He *had* to be okay! "Even if he is, it's only the beginning of winter! It's going to snow and…there'll be lots more cold nights…" She looked up at Jim, pleading. "What can I do?"

"Let me think about it," Jim said.

Then the football game was on. Katie watched him watching it. She wondered if he was thinking. It didn't look much like it. He stared at the screen. The only thing he said was "Way to go, Marino!"

Katie had just about given up on Jim when he turned to her during the commercial. "A doghouse," he said.

"A doghouse?"

"You'll have to ask Farrow if you can put one in the yard. I don't see why not."

Katie was surprised. "Are we gonna buy a doghouse?"

That would be great. A doghouse for Lucky!

"Not buy it," Jim said. "Make it."

"Now that's a real busman's holiday." Mom laughed. "When would you have time?"

"I don't. Katie does."

"*Me?*"

"I'll show you how," he said.

"You're not expecting Katie to make one!" Mom said.

"Why not?"

"For one thing, I don't want her using tools. She could hurt herself. Cut herself or smash her fingers or… Honestly, it's too much for her."

"It's too hard," Katie said. How in the world was she supposed to build a doghouse?

"I can teach her the right way to use a hammer and saw," Jim said.

"Jim, you're forgetting, she's eleven years old," Mom said.

"That's no reason she can't learn, is it?"

"I don't think I could make a doghouse," Katie said. Some of the teenage boys in the building took shop in school and all they made was cheeseboards.

Jim shrugged. "Depends on how much you want it." The commercial was over and he turned back to the game.

She didn't even know how to make a cheeseboard! Kids couldn't even take shop until junior high! Jim Grady was crazy.

But the idea of a doghouse for Lucky was going round and round in her mind. It would keep him dry. It would get him through the winter. It was the only answer.

"Jim?" she asked softly.

"Yeah?" His attention was on the TV.

"You're a carpenter, you know how, so it would be easy as anything for you. I'd help; I'd hold things for you and stuff. You could do it real fast—it wouldn't take you any time at all. Please?"

"No, I'm working two jobs as it is." His eyes were glued to the game. "I'd get you started. The rest is up to you."

She studied his profile. His expression hadn't changed at all. He wasn't a bit sorry he was putting this big load on her. She thought, Jim Grady is a hard-hearted man.

CHAPTER NINE

Katie got into her bed behind the screen in the living room. When it was her bedtime, Mom and Jim Grady would always turn the TV down low. She'd still hear it, but it was like a soothing murmur. She never had any trouble falling asleep.

But tonight she couldn't sleep for anything. She curled up into a ball under the covers and felt an ache deep inside. It was terrible for Lucky to be all alone, wet and freezing. It was terrible for all the homeless people in the city and all the stray cats and dogs, too. It wasn't supposed to be like that! It wasn't fair! She felt bad for everybody, but she *knew* Lucky. She *knew* how he was suffering. She clutched her pillow tight and cried softly, softly so no one could hear.

She thought of praying for Lucky to make it through the night. "Please, God" was all she could whisper before she dozed off, into dreams of icy snowdrifts and a voice helplessly calling for her...

"Katie?" Jim Grady said. "You know that big carton the couch cushions came in? I'll go to the junkyard and throw it over the fence. It's only cardboard, but it might help."

His voice drifted toward her from the dark. She was seeing snowdrifts, whirling and whirling like tornadoes.

"Maybe it won't get drenched through. The sleet's pretty much let up," Jim Grady's voice said.

"Uh-huh," she murmured into her pillow.

Then there was Mom's voice. "Wake up, honey! Come on, Katie, you'll be late for school."

She rubbed her eyes. It felt as though there was sand under her eyelids. She went to the window and looked out. The sidewalk was still wet in patches. Jim Grady talking to her had to have been a dream; there was no way he'd go out in a storm with a cardboard carton. But at least the sleet had stopped. That was something.

"Stop dawdling, Katie. You're late," Mom called.

She brushed her teeth and got dressed. She couldn't find her socks. Everything felt like slow motion.

"What's the matter, honey? Let me look at you." Mom put her hand under Katie's chin. "Are you feeling all right?"

"I'm okay. Just sleepy."

Jim Grady had already left for work. She wouldn't have asked him about it, anyway. She couldn't even ask Mom. It was embarrassing to have Jim Grady come into her dreams.

"Well then, shake a leg!"

She'd find out for sure when she looked in the junkyard.

But then she was *really* late and there wasn't time to go the St. Francis Street way. There wasn't even time to finish breakfast; she ran to school eating her last piece of toast. She ate too fast and it left a big lump in her stomach.

Everything went wrong in school, right from the beginning. Mrs. Ryan didn't yell at her—she never yelled—but she looked at her wristwatch when Katie came in, shook her head, and frowned.

"Just sit down quietly. You're disturbing the class."

"Yes, ma'am," Katie mumbled as she struggled out of her parka. She'd forgotten to take the bunny cap off before she entered the school. She pulled it off quickly, but not before Daniel yelled out, "Whoo-eee, nice hat!"

She'd never, ever wear it again, no matter what!

At lunch, Damita sat with her, Crystal, and Meg. All they talked about was boys. Damita was the one who started it. She was boy-crazy because she had a teenage sister who went out on dates. But Crystal and Meg chimed right in, too.

"Look at that Daniel over there. He's *blazing!*" Damita said. "You know what? My mom said I can have a boy-girl party. I'm gonna do it, too! I'll invite him and Leroy and—"

"You think they'll come?" Meg asked breathlessly.

"I'll tell them I'm having pizza and stuff."

Katie didn't think a boy-girl party would be good at all. Boys could wreck a party in a minute.

Damita, Crystal, and Meg kept going on and on about it. Katie was worried about Lucky, but she couldn't say anything. "You're always talking about that old junkyard dog," Crystal had said one day—not in a mean way, but she *had* said it. So Katie ate her macaroni-and-cheese and didn't say a single word.

She hurried to the junkyard right after school. She was afraid of what she would find there. Lucky could be sick, or even frozen to death! She couldn't keep the terrible pictures out of her mind. She ran the last block.

Then she was at the fence, out of breath. There was a big cardboard carton! Sort of caved in, but it was there. And Lucky's excited bark as he ran toward her was the very best sound in the world.

"Jim Grady did that for you," she said in wonder. "He cares about you, too." It seemed like anything was possible—maybe even a doghouse.

Mr. Farrow was in the junkyard today. That was good—here was her chance.

"Mr. Farrow!" she called. "Mr. Farrow!"

"What now?"

"Is it okay if I put a doghouse in the yard?" This time she wasn't so scared about asking. When you did something once, she thought, it got easier the next time.

"What? What doghouse?"

"The one I'm going to make."

He laughed at her. "You're going to make a doghouse?"

"That's right."

"Out of what? Crepe paper and sticks? I don't want you littering here. This ain't no playground."

"A real doghouse! Out of wood! Jim Grady's a carpenter, and he'll help me." She wanted to say that it was cruel to keep a dog without shelter, but she knew that would only make him mad. "Is it okay? It won't take up any room. It'll look nice."

"What's the matter with that Jim Grady? He don't have nothing else to do?"

Katie swallowed; it was going to be her job, not his. Jim had said that plain and clear.

"Is it okay?" she asked.

"I guess." He shook his head. "Crazy," he muttered.

Now she had permission. Katie sighed. But permission didn't mean a thing by itself. There was no doghouse. It was only an idea in her head.

CHAPTER TEN

"First thing to do," Jim Grady said, "is design it."
He handed Katie a pencil and a piece of graph
paper.

"I never designed anything."

"Come on, think. How do you want it?"

"I don't know. I don't know about doghous-
es." She'd never seen one except on TV.

"Well, what if you were a nice medium-size
dog?" Jim said. "What would you like?"

"I'd like a *big* house. A doggy mansion. And a
fireplace to curl up in front of, to keep me warm,
and—" She stopped herself; she was getting too
silly in front of him.

"That makes sense," Jim said. "It oughta be

big enough for him to stand up comfortably and
have room to turn around. But you want it
warm, too. It should be snug enough to hold his
body heat; too large won't keep him warm. Do
you know his size?"

She knew Lucky as well as she knew anything.
She put her hand against her hipbone. "His head
comes to right here on me."

Jim tossed a wooden ruler toward her. "Figure
out the measurements. You want a little extra all
around, not too much. Put it on the graph paper;
one square for each foot is an easy way to scale it.
What else do you want?"

Katie bit her lip. "What else?"

"You think it should have a roof?"

"Of course! So the rain and snow won't get
in."

"You don't want rain and snow standing on it,
so how do you think it should go?"

Katie thought for a moment. "It should be
peaked? So the water can run off?"

"Good," Jim said.

"It'll be waterproof, right?"

"Right. Primer and two coats of exterior
paint should do it."

"I guess the entrance should be small. To hold
his body heat, like you said."

Jim Grady nodded. "So we'll skip the picture windows."

Katie smiled. "How about window boxes? I'll plant morning glories."

"Maybe someday we'll put curlicues on it. For now, better keep it simple—that dog is out there waiting for it."

There wasn't any time at all, Katie thought. It was sunny today but still very cold. She had heard that the river was icing over. Every day that went by was a hardship for Lucky.

"How long will it take?" she asked.

"Depends on how much work you put in," he said. "And how basic it is."

"If it's not basic, what else would it have?" Katie asked.

"Well, if you have overlapping roof boards, that's better for keeping rain out. But they're more work than a plain roof; it would take longer. You have to decide."

"What would you do?"

"My personal feeling is if you're gonna do something, you may as well do it right."

"I want overlapping roof boards," Katie said.

She had to get started right away. The next big rain or snow could come anytime.

Mom came home from work while Katie was

measuring against her jeans.

"What in the world are you doing?" Mom said.

"Designing Lucky's doghouse."

Mom looked at Jim and then at Katie. Her expression was doubtful.

"It's easy," Katie said. "You think about what it needs, and then the design follows right along."

"That's the truth." Jim was grinning.

Katie finished taking the measurements for the sides before dinner. After dinner, she drew them on the graph paper. She counted the graph boxes carefully. Then, just to be sure, she measured the lines she had drawn. One square to one foot. She measured against her leg again. It came out just right, with a little room to spare.

"Don't you have any homework?" Mom said.

"This is like schoolwork," Katie answered. "We're doing ratios in school."

"You'd better get started on your *real* homework."

"I will, in a minute."

If you were using math for something real, she thought, it was interesting.

Katie interrupted Jim Grady at the TV. She handed him the graph paper.

"Looks fine," he said. He took the pencil and

Katie watched, amazed, as it flew across the paper. He drew the doghouse from a different angle and from the top. "Now you can see exactly how it's supposed to be. This is your blueprint."

Jim Grady knew his business. He was *good!*

"I'll bring some wood from the shop tomorrow. All you have to do is cut it and put it together."

Oh, was that *all* she had to do?

"But I can't—" she started.

"How do you know you can't before you try?" Jim said. "Maybe you can do more than you think."

She hoped Jim Grady was right.

CHAPTER ELEVEN

After school the next day, Damita, Crystal, and Meg were talking about the boy-girl party again. They were excited and Katie felt out of it. She was glad it was far off; she didn't care if it *never* happened.

"You know what we oughta do? We oughta get made over," Damita said. "So we'll be perfect at the party."

Meg clapped her hands. "Oh good, let's!"

"Let's go to my house," Damita said. "We can use my big sister's stuff."

Just the other day, when Katie and Mom were at Woolworth's, they saw some girls her age with makeup plastered all over their faces. Mom shook her head and said, "I don't know how their mothers let them out like that!" Now Damita was saying they were supposed to use her sister's stuff.

"You mean mascara and powder and glop?" Katie asked. Mom wouldn't like that, not one bit.

"Not only that." Damita glanced at her impatiently. "I'm talking about a *complete* makeover. Like in the magazines."

Katie wasn't sure what a complete makeover would be. Anyway, she didn't want one. She looked at Crystal.

Crystal didn't catch her look at all. "Great," she said to Damita, "your house."

Katie wished they were doing something fun instead. This might be her last chance to hang out. Jim Grady would be bringing wood home tonight. Then she'd be busy working on the doghouse in the afternoons.

"How about...anybody want to go skateboarding?" Katie asked.

"No, we're going to Damita's," Meg said.

"Okay!" Damita said. "Let's roll!"

"Okay!" Crystal and Meg echoed.

"Okay," Katie said weakly.

Damita led the way and Katie trailed along. Damita lived in a five-story red-brick building on the other side of the school. It was still the Mud Flats, but lots nicer than the projects; the front door lock wasn't smashed and the intercom worked. There wasn't an elevator, but it was okay to walk up the three flights to Damita's apartment. She followed along behind Crystal and Meg.

Katie wasn't allowed to use the stairs at her building because anybody could come in and hang out there. Once there had been a man hiding on the stairs and he'd hurt a girl even younger than Katie. Mom said to always use the elevators, even if one of them was broken and she had to wait a long time. And Mom said to wait for the next one if she didn't like the looks of somebody already in there. Katie knew to check the little mirror in the back of the elevator, in case somebody was hiding by the side of the door. She could tell right away that Damita's building was a good one. There was no graffiti on the walls, and the stairs didn't smell bad, either.

Inside Damita's apartment was just as nice as outside. Damita had a dining area off the living room, where the couch's red-and-green flowered slipcover exactly matched the curtains.

Damita took them through a narrow hall. She pointed. "That's my parents' bedroom and that's my brothers'."

"How many brothers?" Meg asked.

"Two. Frank is sixteen and Lloyd goes to Community."

This apartment was big!

Damita shared a room with her older sister. There were twin beds with pink bedspreads. There was even a dressing table! It had a three-way mirror on top and a ruffly white skirt; a cute little stool had a matching skirt.

Crystal flopped down on one of the beds. She was acting as though she'd been there before. Katie sat stiffly on the very edge.

Damita spread out her sister's cosmetics. She read out the names of the lipsticks: Apricot Allure, Lilac Fantasy, Goldpearl Bronze, Midnight Red, Hot Toffee.

Meg fingered the cylinders. "Let's put them on!"

"No, wait," Damita said. "We're doing *makeovers*. First, we have to go one at a time and tell the good features and the bad features."

Katie's stomach clutched. She didn't want

anybody talking about her bad features. Especially Damita.

"Everybody has to say their honest opinions," Damita continued.

"All right," Meg said.

"We have to tell the honest truth, for your own good," Damita said.

Katie hated everything about this.

"Crystal first," Damita said.

"I don't want to be the first one." Crystal sounded nervous.

"It's okay, don't worry," Damita said. "You're the prettiest."

Everyone looked at Crystal.

"You have to stand up," Damita said. She was so bossy!

Crystal reluctantly got to her feet. The others sat on the beds and stared at her.

Katie didn't know what she was supposed to say. Crystal was just Crystal. Her friend.

Meg fingered the bedspread. She kept looking over at Damita.

Damita finally started. "Your eyes are nice, 'cause they're so big. You've got long eyelashes, too."

"That's right," Meg chimed in.

"So that's your good feature, and you oughta wear lots of eyeshadow and mascara to show them off," Damita said.

"That's right," Meg said.

"And you have the best hair," Damita said.

Crystal did have beautiful hair; it was long and blond, and fell in waves all by itself.

Crystal looked pleased.

"The bad thing is, your nails look raggedy. You have to grow them for the party," Damita said.

"I'll try to stop biting." Crystal anxiously examined her hands.

"The way they are, nail polish won't even do any good." Meg turned to Damita. "Right?"

"I'll *try*," Crystal said.

"Just stop, that's all," Damita said.

"I don't know if I can." Crystal looked distressed.

"Who cares about nails?" Katie said. This was stupid. "Let's do something else."

Damita shot her a look. "I'll go next."

Damita didn't just stand in front of them. She was twirling around and vogueing.

Everyone said Damita had the best skin. It was smooth, without any zits or freckles. And Meg thought she looked the sexiest; Crystal agreed.

"Except that you're too short," Meg said.

"I am not too short!"

"I'm sorry," Meg said, "but you said to tell the truth. That's all I'm doing, for your own good."

"I'm not short, I'm *petite*," Damita said angrily. She gave Meg a dark look, and her next words sounded like a threat. "Okay, Meg! You're next."

"Anyway, height can't be made over," Katie said. She didn't mean anything bad by that, but Damita glared at her, too.

Everyone liked Meg's smile because she had dimples, but then Damita said her hair was bad. It was frizzy and messy. And she was too chubby. And she'd better go on a diet right away.

Meg looked as though she was about to cry. "But I have dimples," she kept repeating.

"All I'm saying is," Damita continued, "you need to lose at *least* ten pounds before the party. And another thing: your jeans are too tight."

"Just these ones, because they're old," Meg said. "And anyway, at least I've got a figure. Katie's built like a pencil."

"The point is, you're overweight," Damita said.

"Let's do Katie now," Meg said.

"I don't want to be done," Katie said.

"She has bad hair, too," Meg said quickly.

"Yeah, but not as bad as yours," Damita said.

Katie's hand went to her head.

"You have to stand up," Damita said.

Katie stood up, her arms hugging her chest. She didn't realize it until Damita told her to drop them.

"Your hair's dull," Damita said.

"You could have a conditioning treatment at the beauty parlor," Crystal said helpfully.

How could she do that? Beauty parlors were expensive!

Damita frowned. "No, it's the color. Dishwater brown."

Dishwater? That made it sound dirty. Her hair wasn't dirty!

"You could bleach it," Damita said. "You ought to do *something* with it."

"Katie has a real nice smile," Crystal said loyally.

"But no dimples," Meg said, "so it's not that good."

Mom has dimples, Katie thought. She wished she'd inherited them. Mom was so pretty, but they didn't look anything alike. She waited for someone to say her eyes were nice. But no one did. Mom always told her she had big, beautiful, shining brown eyes.

Everyone was studying her.

"What about my eyes?" Katie said hopefully.

"What about them?" Damita said. "They're regular eyes, that's all."

"Oh." Mom liked to make things sound better than they were. Anyway, your own mother's opinion of your looks didn't count for a thing.

"Look at the way you're standing," Damita said.

"Your shoulders droop," Meg said.

Katie wanted to curl up and disappear.

"You come into a room like you're trying to hide," Damita said. "You're awkward. Remember that day you came to school late? You flopped into your seat and dropped your books and... You know what you need? You need *attitude*."

Katie wanted to go home, but she stood there, trapped, like an opossum paralyzed by headlights. There was a sweet-perfume smell in the room that made her feel sick.

"You look too babyish." Damita frowned. "You shouldn't wear that cap with the rabbits."

"I don't anymore. That day was the last time."

"It's not Katie's fault," Crystal said. "Her stepfather won't let her get a new one."

"That's not why! My Grandma knitted it and

I didn't want to hurt her feelings."

"If you'd at least stand up straight—" Damita started.

Katie's lips formed a stubborn line. "I stand the way I stand."

"If you don't listen, we can't fix your looks," Damita said.

"I don't care. This is dumb." That perfume smell was giving her a headache.

"You need a *lot* of fixing, and we're just trying to help," Damita said.

"I don't want help," Katie said.

"You're a bad sport, that's all," Meg said. "Everyone else listened."

"Come on, Katie," Crystal said.

Katie sighed. "All right. What?"

"Your eyebrows don't arch," Damita said. "I'll do them."

Damita pulled a hair out of Katie's eyebrow with her sister's tweezers and it hurt like anything.

"No!" she yelled. "No more!"

Damita sniffed. "Okay, if you don't want to be beautiful."

The whole afternoon was terrible. Katie kept bumping into the furniture. Her feet and hands felt miles too big. Midnight Red on her lips was all wrong. It made them look like clown lips. There was *nothing* about her that felt good. Crystal had the best eyes and hair, Meg had the best smile, Damita had the best skin *and* attitude. She didn't have a best anything. Being good at basketball didn't count at all anymore.

She couldn't wait to leave.

On her way home, Katie wiped the lipstick off. Her feet dragged on the sidewalk. She didn't want to go to any boy-girl party. She was too ugly to be made over.

She headed for the junkyard. Lucky ran toward her as soon as she came near the fence; he was always excited to see her. He didn't care about her hair.

"I don't have your dinner yet," she said. "I'll go home and get it in a minute."

Lucky looked at her with his big, dark eyes. His heart was in his eyes; he loved her, no matter what.

"I just wanted to stop off and see you. Just for company. Lucky, I'm so miserable!"

He was anxiously concentrating on every word. He was miserable, too, and he was such a sweet, smart dog. It wasn't fair!

"Oh, Lucky," Katie said. "I'm doing the very best I can."

He heard the sadness in her voice and tried to lick her hand through the links. She wanted so badly to hug him and hold on tight to a warm, furry body. She sat on the sidewalk next to the fence for a long, long time. She wasn't sure who was comforting whom.

CHAPTER TWELVE

"I'll go get your dinner now." Katie moved away from the fence.

Lucky whimpered and pressed against the links. It seemed like he needed company even more than food and water.

"I'll be right back," she promised.

He followed her along the fence as long as he could. He looked so sad. Maybe instead of the dry dog food she could get him a treat. But what? There weren't any leftovers from last night's ham. Jim Grady had made it, country ham with red-eye gravy, and they'd finished it all up. Jim Grady knew how to cook, too!

The butcher store, Katie thought. Maybe they

had leftovers. Maybe she could even get a great fat bone, big enough for Lucky to chew on. But she didn't know the butcher. Mom never shopped there because the supermarket was cheaper. They might chase her out. Maybe even yell at her.

But then, in her head, Katie could hear Jim Grady's voice as clear as anything. "You got to learn to ask for what you want." That had worked with Mr. Farrow, hadn't it?

At the butcher's, Katie stopped and looked through the glass door. Good, it was almost empty, just one customer talking to the man behind the counter.

A little bell rang as she opened the door. The man looked up for a second as she came in. Then he went on talking to his customer. She waited near the entrance. She looked down at the black-and-white tile floor, worrying about how she would ask.

"Katie? You coming in or what?"

She started. There was *Daniel,* holding a broom and coming straight toward her.

"What are you doing here?" she said.

"This is my dad's store," he said proudly. "I help out. So what d'you want?"

"I was…uh…" If she had money with her,

she would've said hamburger or something and gotten away fast. She took a step backward.

"What?" Daniel said.

"I was…Are there any scraps like leftovers or like a big bone or—" She was mumbling. This was a big mistake.

Daniel laughed. "What's the matter? The relief check late? You making soup to go with the government cheese?"

Her face got hot. "We're not on relief! We don't need your stupid scraps!"

"So what do you want them for?"

"None of your business!" She hated Daniel! "I was asking for the dog, that's all. Never mind. Just go back and sweep!"

He leaned on the broom. "What kind of dog you got?"

"I don't know what kind."

"You don't even know?"

"The junkyard dog. Over at Farrow's junk-yard."

"Yeah, I know the one you mean. You been feeding him?"

"Yes. So what?" Katie looked him right in the face and gave him her most evil look. He was going to make fun of her, she knew it. He was just the kind of kid who would tease Lucky.

"Yeah, I'm sorry for him, too. That Farrow's a mean dude," he said. "Wait a minute. We might have something."

He went around to the back. The customer left. The butcher glanced over at her.

Daniel came back with a brown paper bag. "There's scraps in here and a shank bone."

"Thanks," she said. She looked in the bag. The bone looked big and heavy. It looked all right for Lucky to chew on. "Thanks a lot."

"Do you feed him regular?"

"Every single day."

"So that's why he's looking better." Daniel scuffed the toe of his sneaker against the floor. "I stop by and see him sometimes. I throw him something every once in a while."

"You do?"

"If I pass that way. Yeah, Thunder's an okay dog."

"Thunder?"

"That's what I call him," Daniel muttered.

"His name is Lucky!"

"Lucky? That's a dumb name."

"It is not! Anyway, that's what he answers to, so you better call him Lucky."

"You can't tell me what to call him. He's not *your* dog."

"He is, too! Sort of. I'm making him a doghouse."

Daniel stared at her.

"Well, I am!"

"Yeah, sure."

"My mom's husband is a carpenter, and he's showing me how."

"Oh. That's good, then. Remember that day it snowed? He sure needed *something*."

"I know," Katie said. "I worried about him all night."

Katie crunched the top of the bag in her fingers. Daniel moved the broom around on the floor.

"So…thanks," Katie said.

"Sure. I'll save stuff for him."

"Okay, great."

The bell rang as she opened the door. Who'd ever think the worst boy in the class could be almost nice?

Jim Grady was already home from work when Katie burst into the house.

"Guess what! I gave Lucky a big shank bone. You should've seen the way he loved it!" She wriggled out of her parka. "Did you bring the wood home?"

"Right there." A board was leaning against the refrigerator.

"I'm all set to start. What's first?"

"First you have a snack. Can't do serious work on an empty stomach."

Katie's mom would have said it was too close to dinnertime; Jim didn't think about things like that. She poured a glass of milk and nibbled on a gingerbread cookie while he spread newspaper over the kitchen table.

"You oughta have a workbench, but we'll make do." He put the wood on the table. "This'll be your practice board. For today, just get used to the tools."

"But I want to get started. I have to get it done soon!"

"I know, but you need to work patient and careful. You don't go to step two until you've finished step one just right."

Katie sighed. She wasn't good at being patient.

"Here's your measuring tape," he continued. "See, the hook grabs the edge of the wood, like this; keep the tape straight and make your pencil mark near the edge of the wood."

Katie nodded. No problem so far.

"Always double-check your measurements.

My daddy used to say, 'Measure twice, cut once.'"

"Did your dad teach you carpentry?"

"Mmm-hmm, just the way I'm showing you."

"Was he a carpenter, too?"

"No, he dug coal until the black lung got him. But he could make any single thing he wanted out of wood. He had golden hands."

"That's what Mom says about you."

Jim nodded, pleased. He was holding what looked like a metal ruler attached at a right angle to a wooden handle. "Now here's your try square. Find your pencil mark and press the handle of the square real hard against the edge of the wood. Then you draw a pencil line along the steel edge."

Katie tried it. Jim told her to keep pressing the handle with her other hand while she drew her line.

"See, now you've got a straight-across line. You're ready to make a perfect saw cut."

So far it was a breeze.

"Did your dad always live with you?" Katie asked.

"My daddy, my mama, and my brothers and sisters. Six of us. Up until I was sixteen and came north looking for work. I wasn't working coal, not me. Now here's the C-clamp; it holds the wood in place for you."

Jim watched while she clamped the board to the table.

"Not tight enough," he said.

It was work to turn the clamp's handle, but she managed.

"All by yourself when you were only sixteen!" Talking to Jim felt easy when she was working alongside him, Katie thought. She didn't feel like she had to fill up all the spaces.

"Yeah, well, I had my share of hard times."

"Like what?"

He just shrugged. After a while he said, "Now this is a crosscut saw."

Katie took a good, long look at Jim Grady. On the outside, he looked as tough as the nails in his toolbox, but she suspected he had some bruises on the inside.

He handed the saw to her. Here goes, she thought, this is the hard part.

"Place the backteeth on your mark. Okay. Now use the thumb of your other hand to guide the blade. Above the teeth, on the smooth part. That's right. Keep your fingers away from the teeth."

Katie held the saw against the wood. Its jagged teeth made her nervous.

"Pull the saw toward you three or four times until you get a groove started. Then you take short sawing strokes."

Katie bit her lip. She tried her very best to get it started, but the saw kept catching.

"A real smooth push-pull," he said. "Take it easy. No quick or jerky moves."

Okay, Katie said to herself, slow and easy. But the saw caught anyway. She tried over and over. When it wasn't catching, the blade part was buckling.

"I can't do this," she said.

Jim Grady was watching her. Nothing was working right. She knew her face was red with embarrassment, and that embarrassed her even more.

She finally got a groove started, but then the saw wasn't going anywhere. It was just stuck in the stupid groove. It was making her so mad! If Jim wasn't right there, she would have banged the saw on the table. It was impossible!

"You're jerking it," Jim said.

She struggled with it some more. It was wobbling all over the place. She blew out an exasperated breath.

"Forget it! I quit!" Whatever had made her think she could build something?

"Easy now—" Jim started.

"It's no use! I can't!"

"There's nothing to prove, Katie. You're learning a new skill, that's all, and it'll take as long as it takes. You don't have to be a natural on the first try."

He came up behind her. He put his arms around her and put his hand on the saw's handle over hers. She relaxed her hand and let Jim guide it. "See? Get the feel of it."

Soon they were cutting a nice straight line together. It was amazing; the saw went through the wood as easy as butter. The fresh, clean smell of the sawdust tickled her nose.

"You're getting it," Jim said. "All you need is practice."

His arms around her felt like a hug.

She practiced sawing by herself. It was harder without him. She made one cut that turned out crooked.

"Try again," Jim said. "Remember, guide the saw with your thumb."

She was getting better. She tried to remember that nice, easy feel, and soon it seemed like she was getting the hang of it.

Working together had loosened Jim's tongue, too. "Sometime I'd like to have my own shop," he said. "For custom-made furniture. I'd design it and make it right, all quality work from start to finish, all hand carving. That's what I'd like. Most of the work you see around is stamped out and sloppy."

Katie thought of the carved decoration on her screen. She'd hardly even looked at it; suddenly, she felt ashamed. That had to have taken real skill and time, that carving. She'd take a careful look at it later and say something about it.

"Take a rest—your arm's getting tired," he said. "You can practice some more after dinner."

Katie took another gingerbread cookie out of the box. She sagged into a chair across from him.

"You better sweep up before Mary Ann gets home and sees all this sawdust."

"I will, in a second."

"Too bad there's no room for a real work-bench."

"Thanks for helping me," Katie said.

"Overtime schedule starts next week, so I won't be getting home till late. I'll help you when I can, but—"

"Do you honestly, truly think I can make a **doghouse?**" Katie asked.

"You've got a head on your shoulders, Katie. **You** can do anything you put your mind to."

Putting her mind to sawing had helped her forget about that awful makeover. And seeing Lucky enjoy his bone so much had made her happy. She'd even made friends with Daniel! She sat up tall and straight. If she put her mind to it, maybe she'd even get *attitude*.

CHAPTER THIRTEEN

When Katie saw Daniel in school the next day, she gave him a big smile and said "Hi." He didn't even look at her. He mumbled "Hi" under his breath, so low she could barely hear him. He kept right on fooling around with the guys.

She backed away, confused and embarrassed. You'd never know that they'd had a conversation. She felt stupid for being friendly.

Damita, Crystal, and Meg talked about the boys at lunch. Katie didn't say a word about Daniel. There was nothing to say. He didn't like her. So what, she didn't care.

On her way home from school, she thought

about stopping at the butcher, but she felt funny about it. Daniel had probably forgotten about saving scraps for Lucky. Anyway, the dry dog food had the right vitamins for a dog. So Katie went straight home and waited for Jim Grady to come back from work.

That afternoon, he showed her how to hammer nails.

"Watch me," he said. "You hold the nail straight up and tap the head gently a couple of times."

Jim didn't explain things too slowly the way Mrs. Ryan sometimes did. He talked straight and clear to her, as though she was grown-up, too.

"Once it's in good enough to stand up by itself, take your fingers away from the nail. Your mama'll be real mad at me if your fingers get flattened! Hammer the nail down with slow, steady swings. Now you try it."

Katie got a nail started okay. But then it began to go at a slant.

"Whoa, there's no race to see how fast you can put it in. Just get it in straight. If it bends, pull it out and start with a fresh one."

She started to pull the nail out with the claw

end of the hammer. It was hard. He showed her how to put a block of wood under the hammer to act as a fulcrum.

"Hey, that works!" Katie said.

On her third try, Katie got a nail in just right, as straight as anything. She liked being in control of the hammer. She got into the rhythm of the swings. She drove a neat row of nails into the practice wood. It felt fine.

"Good work," Jim said.

"You're a good teacher, Jim Grady."

He smiled.

"Can I start on the real wood soon?" Katie asked. "It's freezing and Lucky needs— "

"Don't see why not. How about tomorrow?"

"Okay!"

"You could practice sawing some more later tonight and I'll show you how to use the surform plane. You'll be all set."

"Show me now."

"No, Mary Ann will be home anytime. We'll need the table for dinner."

He got up and started putting the tools back in his box.

"I wish we didn't have to put everything away each time," Katie said. She took the newspaper off the table. She folded it so the bits and pieces of wood scraps wouldn't fall out.

"You're right, there oughta be a place to keep things out. This apartment's a sardine can. Too small for three people to move without bumping!"

Katie was surprised by how angry he sounded.

"You oughta have a room of your own," he said.

"It's okay," Katie said. "It's not so bad. That screen you made me, it's good."

"We need a backyard."

"A backyard?" What was he talking about?

"With a couple of trees and some grass underfoot. I'm not made to be cooped up in a little concrete box. This ain't the way to live." He half-laughed. "Never mind, it's 'cause I'm a country boy."

"There's a tree out in front near the playground," Katie said.

"Poor scraggly thing doesn't know it's a tree. Probably thinks it's an overgrown hydrant."

He handed her the broom and then got the dustpan. He knelt down while she swept up a little pile of sawdust.

"You don't like it here," Katie said.

"Not especially."

"Oh."

Katie couldn't tell what he was thinking from his deadpan expression. He sounded so restless with all his talk about trees and grass. And just when she'd made friends with him and was getting to like his company!

The next afternoon, Jim Grady gave Katie a piece of good wood to cut for one side of the doghouse. She was afraid of spoiling it. She was glad Jim was there. She checked her measurements over and over. Then she drew her pencil line against the try square. She took the saw in her hand and hesitated.

"Go ahead," Jim said. "You're ready."

Katie bit her lip. She started the cut. She worked on keeping the saw straight. Slow and easy, she reminded herself.

It took her a long time. When she finished, there was a nice straight edge. A big smile broke out on her face.

"After I finish the doghouse, maybe I'll make something else!"

"There's a way to go yet. You got to cut and sand all the sides. Then the roof boards. Then I'll teach you how to nail it together."

"Okay."

Katie smoothed off the sawed edge with the surform plane. It looked like a cheese grater, she thought, but it had hundreds of razor-sharp cutting edges. Sawdust flew all over the place. The sweet fresh-wood smell made her think of trees and leaves and sunshine.

"Remember, next week I'm starting overtime and you'll be on your own," Jim said. "I told your mama you're responsible and you can handle it. So use the tools right and watch what you're doing. Don't make a liar out of me."

"I won't."

"Listen, if you get stuck, wait for me to come home."

"Mom's worried, right?"

"Well, she's...protective of you."

"You think she babies me too much?"

"She took care of you all on her own, all through some bad times. So maybe she goes overboard keeping you out of harm's way. I don't know. All I know is what I'm seeing with my own two eyes. You can do carpentry, Katie."

Katie stood up straight. "I know I can."

"Okay then." They grinned at each other.

Then Jim showed her how to use a keyhole saw. It had a really skinny blade with a super-sharp point that could start a cut from a tiny drilled hole. It was for cutting curves. She'd need it when she was ready to make the entrance to the doghouse.

He wrapped a piece of sandpaper around a block of wood. "See, here's your sander. First use coarse paper, then fine. It'll take longer than an electric sander, but I promised your mama, nothing electric."

"That's a waste of time," Katie said. "I'd be careful."

"I know, but hey, we don't want to get Mary Ann too uptight. Let's go along with her on this." Then he showed her how to get the most out of each stroke.

"I wish you weren't working late next week," she said.

"It's good overtime," Jim said. "I'm lucky to get it. We're renovating an apartment downtown; lots of work for the whole crew."

He seemed content, but later, when she was in bed, she heard him and Mom talking. Katie could tell Mom didn't like any part of it.

"I'll never get to see you," Mom said.

"It's not forever."

"At least quit the night watchman."

"No. No, I'm making some real money."

"We can wait a while." Mom sounded upset.

"Can't we just relax, and, all right, so it'll take a while longer, but—"

"Yeah, and watch the months turn into years. No, I'm not about to wait one extra day I don't have to."

"It's not that bad here."

"The hell it ain't!"

They were fighting. Katie clutched her pillow to her chest.

"When are you supposed to sleep?" Mom said.

"That's my problem."

"You are the most stubborn…!"

"I'll do what I have to."

"We're supposed to *discuss* things, aren't we?" Mom said.

Their voices were getting louder. The sharp, stabbing sounds put a knot in Katie's stomach.

"We got married to be together, didn't we?" Mom was good and mad. "What did we get married for?"

"That's a real dumb question, Mary Ann!"

"You can't work all the time!"

"Don't tell me what I can't do."

"Am I *ever* going to see you?"

Then the bedroom door slammed and Katie couldn't hear them anymore. All the yelling had left her with a real bad feeling.

Yesterday, he'd just about said he hated living here with them. Maybe he was planning to work so much because he didn't want to come home and be with Mom anymore. Jim Grady kept things to himself; you couldn't tell what he was thinking. Maybe all his talk about overtime was an excuse to be staying out. On TV, when the man started working late every night, that was a sure sign of trouble. Katie hoped he wasn't fixing to leave right away. She needed his help. She'd better learn *everything* about making a doghouse just as fast as she could.

She should have known better than to expect much from Jim Grady. Or from Daniel. They were bound to let her down. Women were there for her to depend on: Mom and Grandma Hattie and Aunt Gloria. That was enough. Men just weren't worth all the hassle and tears.

Aunt Gloria's man played the trumpet and he was always going off on tour. That's what he said, anyway. He disappeared for months. She'd even overheard Mom talking: "My sister's blind 'cause no tour is *that* long."

If Katie's own father could walk out without a backward glance, anybody could.

CHAPTER FOURTEEN

On Saturday, while Jim Grady was sleeping, Katie sawed the other sides of the doghouse by herself.

Mom shook her head when she saw the bits of wood flying all over her clean kitchen floor.

"I'll sweep it up later," Katie said.

Mom watched while Katie started a new cut.

"Careful, Katie. Your fingers!"

"I know how. Don't worry."

When Jim woke up in the afternoon, he came in to see how she was doing.

"You got a lot done."

"All four sides! I'm ready for the keyhole saw."

"You remember how to use it?"

"I'm not sure."

"Come on, let's do it together." He helped her saw the curve for the entrance. His arms were around her again. It wasn't like a hug, Katie told herself. It was just for sawing.

"Now that's beginning to look like a real doghouse," Mom said.

"Didn't I tell you, Mary Ann?" Jim winked at Katie. "Now you're up to the roof boards. Measure real careful—they have to fit just right. They're thicker; so they'll be tricky to cut."

"What's after that? Show me everything I have to do."

"Everything? All at once?"

"So I'll know what to do when you're not here," Katie said. She was going to get this doghouse finished!

"Okay. You'll cut the floor and the blocks to hold it off the ground. You'll smooth off the sides and ends with the surform plane. Then you'll sand everything down, coarse and fine; you want a nice smooth finish. Next comes nailing everything together. I'll show you how to overlap the roof boards."

Katie listened carefully. If she thought of one step at a time, it didn't seem so impossible.

On Sunday, Katie cut the roof boards. There were ten of them. It took a long time. She was nervous about measuring right; she re-measured a couple of times for each one. When she finished, she held her breath and lined them up. They all matched!

Jim woke up late in the afternoon. He came into the kitchen, stretching and yawning.

"I heard sawing in my sleep," he said.

"I'm sorry," Katie said quickly.

"That's okay. Don't they have sawing noises for sleep in the cartoons? Bzzz, bzzz, bzzz."

"Let's get the table cleared off now," Mom said.

"Not yet! It's not dinnertime yet!" Katie said.

"You've been at this all day," Mom said. "Why don't you go out and play?"

"When you're tired is when you make mistakes," Jim said.

"How do I nail it together?"

"You've still got a lot of sanding to do first."

"I know, but tell me what comes after. I want to know. In case you're away when I get up to it."

"Right, I start overtime tomorrow. I won't be here much."

"That's an understatement," Mom muttered.

Jim marked the places where the nails would go on the sides and where the sides would be attached to the bottom. He marked the wood that would make the roof's peak.

"How do I attach the roof boards?"

He held the boards and showed her how they would go. "Have each one overlap by half an inch. You want them tight to keep the rain out."

"Okay." She listened hard, frowning with concentration. "What else?"

"That's enough for now," Jim said. "That's enough to keep you busy for a while."

He started to stack the wood in the corner. Katie was careful about putting his tools back in the toolbox; she didn't want to get him mad.

He noticed and smiled.

He was acting nice, Katie thought. Sometimes men were nice to you and the next minute, they didn't know you.

When Katie went to feed Lucky, she could see someone at the junkyard fence from down the block. It sure looked like—it was—Daniel!

She walked over slowly. Lucky was chewing on something.

"What are you doing here?" she asked.

Daniel turned to her, grinning. "I gave him a bone. Look at him, he loves it!"

"Well, I have his regular food. It has all the

vitamins and stuff." She knelt down to slip the pan under the fence. Lucky looked up at her gratefully, but kept right on crunching the stupid bone.

"Hey, how come you didn't come by the store? I was saving scraps."

"Oh. I thought you forgot about that."

"Why would I forget? I said I'd save them, didn't I?"

Katie shrugged.

Daniel stuck his hands deep in his jacket pockets. "Man, it's getting cold!"

Katie nodded. The wind was cutting through her jeans.

"So how's the doghouse coming?"

"I'm working on it."

"You better hurry up. Thunder needs it."

"Lucky!"

"Okay, okay, Lucky."

"That keyhole saw's pretty tricky." She'd bet anything he didn't even know what it was.

"Yeah, by the time you get done, it'll be spring," he said.

"I might be finished next week!"

"Well, the dog needs it now."

"I said I'm working on it. That's more than you're doing!"

Daniel shifted his weight. "I was just saying I bet he's cold right now."

"I got it all cut out. You should see how perfect I did the roof boards."

"What are you up to now?"

"Sanding. That'll take a while, because it's just sandpaper, I mean, not electric. But after that, I have all the pieces cut out and—"

"How come you don't have an electric sander? I thought your dad was a carpenter."

"My mom's husband isn't going to be around that much, and she doesn't want me using electric stuff by myself." That sounded so babyish. Katie tucked her chin into her collar.

"Yeah, I know, moms are like that."

They stood at the fence and watched Lucky. Daniel didn't say anything. Katie couldn't think of anything to say. If Damita was standing right here, she'd be flirting like anything. Katie didn't know how to flirt. Even if she could think of one word, it wouldn't come out through the thickness in her throat.

Lucky left the bone and gobbled up the dog food. Katie watched him. When he finished, she knelt down and picked up the pan. She poured water from the carton into it. Every move she made felt slow and awkward, as if her hands belonged to a stranger.

"Um, I guess he needs water," Daniel said.

"Uh-huh."

She slid the filled pan back under the fence. "Well, good-bye, Lucky. See you tomorrow."

She would have liked to sit down and talk to Lucky for a while, but not with Daniel standing right there.

She started to walk away. She felt Daniel watching her back. It was like she was just learning to walk, like her feet didn't know which way they were supposed to move. Being around a boy felt awful!

"Hey, Katie!"

She turned back. "What?"

"I was thinking. I could, uh, I could help you sand. Like it'll go faster."

"I guess."

"Twice as fast," Daniel said. "At least. So?"

"So what?" Katie asked.

"So is it okay?"

"I guess."

"All right! I'll come by tomorrow afternoon. Sometime after school."

"Okay."

"So, uh, where do you live?"

"In the projects."

"I know. What apartment?"

"Four B in Building One."

"Four B in Building One," he repeated.

The only reason he'd be coming over was for Lucky's sake, Katie thought. But she felt a funny glow starting in her chest and moving right up to her face. Maybe he'd say hi to her in school tomorrow.

CHAPTER FIFTEEN

At school the next day, Daniel didn't act anything like a friend. This time, Katie was more careful; she waited for him to say hi first, but he didn't. She passed right in front of him on the way to the lockers. She was no more than twelve inches from his nose, but he acted as if she was invisible.

It wasn't a good day. She saw Crystal and Damita passing notes in class. Crystal was supposed to be Katie's best friend. Damita made Katie feel left out.

At recess Damita said, "Crystal and me are gonna have lots of dates when we get to junior high. We're the type." Katie and Meg were standing right there, but Damita didn't say anything about *them*.

"What do you mean, the type?" Katie asked.

Damita shrugged. "The type that gets lots of dates, that's all. Like my big sister."

The boys were standing across the yard. Daniel and Leroy and those guys.

"Let's go talk to them," Damita said.

"No!" Meg said. "We can't!"

"What are we going to say?" Crystal asked.

"I don't know," Damita said. "Look at the cute way Daniel's hair falls on his forehead. Jet black's the best hair color on a boy."

"It is?" Meg asked.

Would Damita think Katie was "the type" too, if she knew Daniel was coming over? But Damita would see right away how he was ignoring her. So Katie didn't say anything.

"Leroy's taller," Meg said.

"But Daniel's the coolest," Damita said. "Let's go invite them to my party."

"Are you *really* going to?" Crystal said.

"I'm having a party. I made up my mind."

"So let's ask them," Meg said.

No one moved.

"Okay, let's do it!" Damita said.

"Now?" Crystal asked.

Damita took a deep breath. "Now or never!"

Damita led the way. Katie followed the other girls, her feet dragging.

"What are you guys doing?" Damita said, as cool as anything. Then the guys were horsing around, nudging each other, and laughing, and Damita and Crystal had big phony smiles and Meg couldn't stop giggling.

"…my party next Saturday…" Damita was saying. "…pizza and superheaters and…"

"Maybe I'll come if you get pepperoni," Eddie said.

"Yeah, I like sausage," Daniel said.

"Well, I'm having all *kinds* of pizza and…" Damita was doing most of the talking.

"So where are you gonna be after school?" Leroy asked.

Damita had her head sort of down and she looked up at Leroy through her eyelashes. "I guess we'll be around the candy store." Then she straightened up and said, rolling her eyes, "Except for Katie. She's busy making a *doghouse.*"

Everybody laughed—John, Leroy, Eddie, Damita, Meg—all of them were looking at her and laughing.

"For that junkyard dog," Damita said, as if it was the funniest thing in the world.

CHAPTER FIFTEEN

Katie's face was flaming hot. With blurred vision, she saw Eddie guffawing, big teeth and open mouth. She saw Daniel looking off into the distance. He didn't say a word. She wanted to disappear, but she was frozen in place.

Everyone was talking and Meg had her stupid giggle.

"So maybe we'll see you," Leroy said.

"Not if we see you first," Meg said, trying to sound snappy like Damita. It came out lame instead.

Then the boys went off to play ball, and Meg whispered to Damita, "I think Leroy likes you."

Damita shrugged and said, "Well, it's going to be D 'n' D."

"What's that?" Crystal asked.

"Damita 'n' Daniel."

On the way back to class, Crystal walked with Katie. "Are you mad?"

"I hate her," Katie muttered. I hate *him*, she thought. I hate him the most!

"She didn't mean anything," Crystal said. "You're being too sensitive. She was just being funny."

"Oh yeah, funny. *Not!*"

"She was nervous about inviting the boys, that's all it was."

"Who cares about her stupid party."

"Come on, be a good sport," Crystal said.

"She needs a big makeover on her brain."

"Don't be like that, Katie."

"Do you *like* her?"

"She's okay. She's nice."

That afternoon, Katie messed up on the social studies test. She couldn't think of the names of the Civil War battles that she'd known as well as her own hand just that morning. It was an altogether terrible day and she couldn't wait to go home.

Katie carried the doghouse pieces from the corner of the kitchen and put them on the table. She wrapped the coarse sandpaper around a block, the way Jim Grady had showed her.

Crystal, Damita, and Meg would be outside the candy store right this minute, she thought. They'd be acting stupid with Leroy, Eddie, and those guys around. And Daniel. He'd be there with them.

She sanded furiously and the sawdust flew. Some of it must have gone into her eyes, because they were kind of tearing. She held the block in both hands and rubbed it back and forth so fast and hard it made her arms ache. In school tomorrow, Damita would be saying how much fun they'd had. She sanded, rubbing the smile off Damita's face. She sanded, wiping out Daniel's grin. "Yeah, I like sausage" was a just plain rude answer to a party invitation. She'd known all along that he wasn't nice.

She was working herself into a sweat and scraping her knuckles on the wood. She stopped and took a breath. She slowed her pace. This was going to take forever. There were so many pieces, and then she'd have to go over all of them again with the fine sandpaper. She wished Jim Grady would be coming home this afternoon to help her. But he wouldn't be.

Why couldn't Mom just say okay to an electric sander? Mom babied her too much, that was the truth. It was time to be more grown-up. She'd have to learn how to say "What are you guys doing?" the way Damita did, cool and easy.

"What are you guys doing?" Katie said to the roof boards. She wiped her face with the bottom of her T-shirt; it left tan sawdust streaks on the fabric.

The doorbell buzzer echoed through the kitchen. Maybe Jim *was* back early and had lost his key or something. She went to the front door and checked to be sure the chain was on.

"Who is it?" she said through the door. She knew never to open it without asking.

"Who is it?" she said again, louder.

"Daniel."

What? She opened the door a crack, letting it bang against the chain. "What are you doing here?"

"Remember, we said—I was gonna sand?"

She could hardly see him. Mostly, she saw the red of his jacket.

"I was gonna help sand?" he repeated.

"Oh."

"What?"

"I said 'oh.'"

"Are you gonna open the door or what?"

She hesitated. "I guess so." She hadn't picked up around the apartment. The screen was folded back from her bed. She tried to remember if she'd left any underwear out. No, it was safely tucked away in the hamper.

She unhooked the chain and opened the door.

"Did you forget about me coming?" he asked.

"I didn't think you were."

"I'm here, right?" He was standing in the doorway. "So are you gonna let me in?"

She'd been blocking the way; she moved over. "All right, come in if you want to."

She led him into the kitchen and nodded at the table. "That's the wood."

"Uh-huh."

Who did he think he was, showing up like nothing happened? Well, now he was here and she didn't know what to do with him. "You can go ahead and sand," she said. "Coarse paper first. You wrap it around the block like this."

"You sawed all those pieces by yourself?" he said.

"Yeah."

"They look good. That's the entrance, right?"

"You do curves with a keyhole saw," Katie said. "It's hard, but I know how."

"Your dad taught you all that? That's cool."

"My mom's husband."

"He's not your dad?"

"No."

"Anyway, it's looking good. Looks like Thund—" He stopped himself and grinned. "Lucky's gonna have a doghouse!"

"You here to talk or to work?" Katie said.

"What's the matter with you?" he said.

"Nothing. You're the one who thinks making a doghouse is so funny."

"Me? What did *I* do?"

Katie shrugged.

He picked up the wrapped block and rubbed it against a board. "Like this?"

"Yeah. You can work sitting down."

He sat down in a kitchen chair and Katie sat down opposite him. He slowly began to sand. Katie went back to the board she had started. The only sound in the kitchen was the *woosh* of the paper against the wood.

"You mean at recess?" He didn't look up; his eyes were fixed on the wood. "*I* didn't laugh."

"You didn't say anything, either."

"What do you want? I'm working with you."

"You could have said so."

Woosh—woosh—woosh.

"What comes after sanding?" he asked.

"I nail it together."

"I bet we could get it done by the end of the week."

"Then I have to put on primer. And paint, two coats. And let it dry good in between. Exterior paint, so it'll be waterproof."

"It can dry overnight, can't it? So we can do the second coat the next afternoon. I bet we can get it done in a week."

"What do you mean, 'we'?" She looked at him through narrowed eyes. "You planning on being here?"

"You want help or not? You want to finish it by yourself?"

"I want Lucky to have it. I don't care *who* works on it."

He made a big thing of looking all around the kitchen. "I don't see nobody else here."

Katie shrugged.

"Listen, I'm doing you a favor!"

"Don't do me any favors," she said.

"Okay, I'm doing a favor for the dog."

"All right, go ahead."

"Wow, thanks a whole bunch," he said. He sounded mad enough to get up and leave any minute. "What's your problem?"

"What's *your* problem? You're sitting right here in my house, but in school you can't even say hello!"

He looked down, uncomfortable. "I said hi."

"No, you didn't. Like it would kill you to say hello. Like you don't know me." Her voice broke. "Like you'd never heard of a house for a junkyard dog. Big joke!"

"I just told you, *I* didn't laugh."

"You want a medal?"

"What did you expect me to do?"

"Oh, nothing!"

He frowned at the wood and got busy sanding.

Katie got busy sanding, too. She'd sounded as if she cared, she knew she did! She could have died. She wished Daniel would disappear.

"You know what would happen?" he mumbled.

"What?"

"Everybody would make a big deal of it. They'd start saying all that stuff. 'Daniel and Katie sitting in a tree, k-i-s-s-i-n-g.'"

Katie knew the rest of it. First comes love, then comes marriage, then comes Katie with a baby carriage. Was he crazy? Nobody in sixth grade would say that!

"You taking a time trip back to kindergarten?" Katie asked.

"Yeah, well. I mean, the guys would be teasing and all that," he mumbled.

Daniel wasn't as cool as everybody thought— Damita should see him now! The idea that Daniel could get embarrassed was amazing.

"So that's why," he finished.

"I don't care, it's not right," Katie said. "If you're friends with somebody, you don't turn it on and off."

"You don't have to get *public* about it," he said.

"You're supposed to stand up for a friend," she said.

He wouldn't look up at her. "Big deal. It wasn't like life or death." He frowned, concentrating on the board.

She ran her fingers across it; it was smooth, he'd done a good job. He was full of surprises; he'd been sitting still and working, not fooling around the way he did in class.

"You want some soda?" Katie asked.

"Sure."

She opened the refrigerator. "We have Pepsi." She handed him a can and took one for herself.

"Thanks." He flipped open the top. She was glad he didn't shake the can to make it spray, the way the boys did at lunch. He was much nicer by himself.

"There's usually cookies, but we don't have any today. We usually do, though."

"That's okay."

"If you're gonna come over tomorrow——what kind of soda do you like?"

"Any kind. Pepsi's good."

Katie opened her can. "I need a break. My arms are falling off."

He grinned. "Mine, too."

Damita was right, Katie thought; he had the looks. He had a smile that could melt butter.

"There's still a lot to do," she said.

"So, we'll get it done." He took a sip. "You're good at woodworking. For a girl."

"What's being a girl got to do with it?"

"I don't know. The other girls get so stupid, they'd cut their fingers off."

"I'm taking shop in junior high next year." She hadn't thought about it before, but that minute she decided for sure.

"You can't. The girls get home ec, and the boys get shop," he said.

"I'm taking shop, no matter what. Even if I have to see the principal!" She could do that, she thought. No one could be scarier than Mr. Farrow.

He gave her a thumbs-up. "Go for it," he said.

There she was, talking to Daniel as easy as anything. But she wasn't going to let herself *really* like him. No way. What good was somebody you couldn't count on?

CHAPTER SIXTEEN

By the time Mom came home, Katie had the kitchen cleaned up. Mom carried a bag of groceries in and wearily put it down.

"Katie! There's sawdust all over this counter!"

"Oh, sorry." She reached for the sponge.

"No, not with the dish sponge," Mom said. She wiped the counter with paper towels. "I'll be glad when this doghouse of yours is done."

"Me too."

When they sat down to dinner, Jim's chair was empty. The table wasn't as crowded. Seemed as if he was never around anymore. Katie finally had a chance to be alone with Mom. That should have been good. But it wasn't.

Mom was very quiet. She ate staring off into space.

"Mom, are you sad?"

"No, honey, just tired. There were more admissions in the hospital today than we normally see in a week." Mom picked up the noodle casserole. "Do you want any more?"

Katie shook her head. There was a big mound on her plate.

"Well, I'll keep it warm for Jim." She got up and put the bowl in the oven.

"He's not eating here," Katie said.

"Just in case he's hungry later." Mom sighed and sat down again.

Katie inhaled Mom's Chanel No. 5. It was *expensive,* not for every day. The fragrance was strong; Mom must have put it on just a little while ago. Maybe Mom was saving dinner for him and trying extra hard—her special perfume and everything!—because she suspected he was about to leave, too.

"Mom, is Jim Grady leaving?"

Mom put her fork down. "Where did that come from?"

"I heard you fighting the other night."

"I was mad about the overtime because I'll miss him, that's all it was. It didn't mean anything."

"Would you miss him a lot? Would you be awful sad if he left?"

"Katie? I thought the two of you were getting along fine. I know you felt shy with him at the beginning and…" Mom chuckled. "…and I think he was sort of shy with you, too. But I thought you were getting to like him."

"I guess," Katie mumbled. "He's okay."

"Then what's all this talk about him leaving? Do you *want* him to?"

"I don't care."

"Oh, honey, you'll get used to him. You'll see, he's wonderful!"

Mom didn't hear the way he was talking about their apartment, Katie thought. She didn't hear his talk about trees and grass. He was itching to go right back to the country where he used to live, and Mom didn't know.

"Now why are you frowning like that?" Mom asked. "Those lines are gonna freeze right between your eyes."

"Was it awful for you when my father left?"

"It was hard," Mom said.

"Were you sad and lonely all by yourself?"

Mom smiled. "I wasn't by myself, you know. You've always been my little ray of sunshine."

"Did you *love* him?"

"Well, I thought I did." Mom buttered a piece of bread. Rye bread. That's what she bought now because it was the kind Jim Grady liked. "We were too young to know anything. He was a nice boy, but…Katie, it was so long ago, it's not worth talking about."

"He wasn't nice. He left you flat with a little baby." Grandma Hattie said that he came and went like a wisp of smoke, without leaving a trace behind.

"I don't want you thinking bad about your father."

"I don't see there's anything good to think."

"No, Katie, that's not so. He had a real nice sense of humor. And he was smart as a whip, just like you. But he was only a boy. Taking care of a family was too much for him."

"But he's not a boy now."

Mom shrugged. "The important thing is he gave you those big beautiful brown eyes."

That wasn't the important thing. Mom was trying to make it sound a lot better than it was. And she wasn't admitting there was trouble with Jim Grady, either.

"How do you know you love Jim Grady?"

"I do." Her face was soft and glowy. "Katie, he's the best thing that ever happened to me. I don't know how I got so lucky."

Mom's heart was going to get broken into little pieces, Katie thought. She'd never hand over her heart to any man; even Aunt Gloria said they all meant trouble.

"Aunt Gloria says, 'Men—you can't live with 'em and you can't live without 'em.'"

Mom shook her head. "My sister says a lot of things. The fact is, you *can* live with them." Then she got a faraway look in her eyes. "And you can live without them, too. If you have to."

Mom knew, Katie thought. She knew, and she was only pretending everything was still all right.

"We can live without them, right?" Katie said. "We used to, just the two of us."

"I don't think I'd *want* to." Mom smiled.

Katie couldn't smile back. She got busy with her noodles. She just couldn't understand grown-ups.

On the next two afternoons, Daniel came over to help. They got all the pieces sanded. They nailed the blocks to the bottom of the floor and then attached the side pieces. They used the special wood glue, too, to make it hold good. And everything fit together perfect! Daniel said, "Hey, it's getting to look like something!" When Daniel gave her a high five, Katie couldn't help grinning back at him.

But then she got stuck. She didn't know how to put the roof boards on. She waited for Jim Grady. It was after ten when he finally walked in the door. He was awful tired, but he sat down with her at the table and explained once again how to overlap them and how they should be attached on top.

"Let Jim be," Mom said. "He needs his rest."

"It's okay, Mary Ann," Jim said. "Katie's done a fine job. I mean it, this is Grade A work. And it didn't take you long, either."

"I had help," Katie said. "A boy from my class came over. Three afternoons."

"Exactly who is this boy?" Mom said. "Why didn't you say anything? You never told me some boy was here."

"Come on, Mary Ann. He must be a nice kid," Jim said.

"He's okay, I guess," Katie said. "There's nothing to tell. I don't really like Daniel. Not really. Not a bit. He likes doing carpentry, that's all."

Jim smiled. "You better get ready, Mary Ann. Before you know it, Katie's boyfriends are gonna be lining up in the hall outside."

"Stop it. She's much too young for boyfriends," Mom said.

"You can't keep her from growing up, any more than you can stop a river running downstream," Jim said.

"There's no need to rush it, either!" Mom looked like she was about to fight with him again.

"I'm not pretty enough for boyfriends," Katie mumbled to herself, but Jim heard.

"Go look in the mirror," he said, "and see that beautiful proud shine on you from doing good work."

Katie had to keep herself from running to the mirror right then.

"Yeah, that's a fact," Jim continued. "You're growing up shining and beautiful, just like your mom."

Katie hoped her flush of pleasure didn't show. Why was he being so nice? The one thing she did know about Jim Grady was that he never sugarcoated a single thing. If he still thought Mom was beautiful, then maybe... Maybe she had been wrong about him. Maybe she'd been imagining things. She felt a warm little flicker of hope—just for Mom's sake.

"Well, I'm taking my shower." Mom got up

and stretched. "Katie, don't forget it's a school night. And Jim has to get to sleep, too."

"Okay," Katie said.

Then it was just her and Jim sitting at the kitchen table.

He was looking over the doghouse. "That dog's gonna have a good shelter. Lucky's the right name for him."

"He's not so lucky," Katie said. "He still lives in that junkyard."

"Well, he's lucky for a junkyard dog because you're helping him."

"You know what I wish? I wish I could give him a bath. And a good brushing, too. His fur is all matted and dirty; you can't hardly tell the color. I bet he's a nice golden brown underneath."

"He could use some care," Jim said.

"He must feel awful itchy. I'll ask Mr. Farrow if I can take him for a day. He might let me. I'll give him a bath. I'll sneak him up here and—"

"You can't bring a dog in."

"I'd be careful. I'd take him up the stairs. If no one sees—"

"No. You know the rules." Then Jim surprised Katie by suddenly slamming his hand on the table. "I am *tired* of this place and all its rules!

Not even room for a man to stretch here."

"It's okay," Katie whispered. "I understand about not bringing Lucky home."

"This ain't no way for a man to live. No way!"

Katie studied his face. She *had* to know for sure. Finally she went ahead and asked him.

"You planning to move on?"

"Damn right I am," he answered in that same angry voice.

So there it was, plain as anything, and no chance of pretending it away. If he was going to leave them, Katie wished he would just hurry up and *go!*

CHAPTER SEVENTEEN

Sunshine was coming around the edges of the screen when Katie woke up on Saturday morning. She stretched lazily and thought it was going to be a beautiful day. Then she remembered. Damita's boy-girl party. That afternoon.

Daniel would be there, but so what? She didn't like anything about boys. But she'd go anyway. Just to see what it was like. It would probably be awful.

At breakfast Mom said, "I'll get to ironing your blue dress in a minute; I'll have it ready in plenty of time."

"You don't have to. Everyone's wearing jeans."

"But it's your party dress. You look so sweet in—"

"Not in sixth grade! No one wears party dresses in sixth grade!"

"Are you sure?"

"Yes. Damita said."

When it was almost time to get ready, Katie suddenly wasn't sure at all. She called up Crystal.

"Jeans," Crystal said.

"Regular, everyday jeans?"

"I'm wearing Jordaches and my new pink sweater, you know the one with the ruffle at the neck? And my mom is lending me her heart locket."

"Oh." Katie bit her lip. "It's at three, right? I'll come by your house at a quarter of."

"I have to go early. I'm helping Damita set everything up."

"Oh."

"So I'll see you there, okay? It'll be so much fun!"

It didn't sound like fun, Katie thought. But— but maybe it would be. If she looked right.

"Mom!" she wailed.

"Sssh, Jim's sleeping."

"I don't care *what* Jim Grady's doing!"

"What's the matter?" Mom said.

"I don't have Jordaches."

"Honey, the only difference is the stitching on

the pockets." Mom smiled. "A couple of different curlicues, that's all."

"But they're *designer* jeans!"

"It doesn't matter."

"It's not the same."

"There's no use worrying about it, just wear what you have." Mom gave her a little hug. "You'll be fine."

Katie washed up carefully. She scrubbed under her nails. She brushed her teeth for the second time and swished full-strength mouthwash around, even though it made her tongue burn. And she mentally went through all the tops in her drawer. Her white sweater was the best one.

When she was all dressed, she studied herself in the mirror. There she was—regular old Katie Lawrence.

"I look like I'm going to school," she complained. "It's a *party*."

"Here. Stand still." Mom put some dabs of her Chanel No. 5 on Katie's earlobes and wrists.

"Thanks! Mom, can I wear your necklace?"

"My necklace?"

"Your pearl necklace. Can I?"

"All right, but don't tug at it. Be careful, okay?" Mom fastened the clasp at Katie's neck. "Well, just look at you!"

The pearls shimmered against the soft white wool; they were beautiful. Katie brushed her hair back; if it would just *stay!*

"Mom, do I look special?"

"Wait, I have a terrific idea. I saved that pretty candy box Jim gave me, and you know what? It has a white satin bow with pearls right in the middle."

White satin. That was glamorous, Katie thought.

Mom got the step-stool and hunted on the top shelf of the closet. "Here it is!" She unwound the wiring attached to the bow and held it against Katie's head. "What do you think?"

"It's so pretty," Katie breathed.

Mom anchored it to Katie's hair with a million bobby pins. It was on the side and it held her hair back the way it was supposed to go.

"There! *Now* you look special."

Pearl necklace, white sweater, white satin with *more* pearls: everything matched. And she was inhaling the delicious perfume all around her.

Katie smiled at herself in the mirror. "I do, kind of, don't I?"

When Damita opened the door, Katie saw right

away that she was wearing makeup. Crystal and Meg were, too! They didn't look as if they had clown lips, either—it was soft pink lipstick. And they all had gray-green eyeshadow, blended in nice. Crystal's eyelashes looked thick and a mile long—she was wearing mascara! Damita's sister must have helped them.

Katie could feel herself shrinking. She could tell by the way Damita was staring at her that she looked all wrong. Nobody was wearing a bow.

The boys were there—Daniel, Eddie, Leroy, and John. They were standing on the other side of the room, with big bowls of potato chips and pretzels. They looked everyday regular, but the other girls seemed so grown-up!

"You all had a makeover," Katie said. She should have asked Mom... Or she should have come early... Or...or something.

Damita laughed. "I guess you have a make-*under!*"

The boys heard them. "Make what?" Eddie yelled.

"Make out!" Leroy yelled.

Daniel was horsing around and laughing. He wasn't noticing her. Not one bit. He didn't even look her way.

Eddie threw a pretzel at Damita.

"Cut it out," she said, but she was smiling at the attention. He threw another one that bounced off her shoulder and onto the maroon rug.

Boys act as if they belong in a stable, Katie thought.

Crystal brought a tray of little sandwiches from the kitchen.

"What's that?" Leroy asked.

"They're good. We made them," Crystal said.

They were pinwheel sandwiches with fillings in different colors that must have taken forever to fix. The boys stuffed them in their mouths three at a time and they were gone in a second.

"Don't leave some for anyone else," Katie said. Men were more trouble than they were worth.

"It's okay," Crystal said. "There's more."

Damita was holding another plate.

Katie looked straight at Daniel. "They still don't have to be pigs."

"Oink, oink," he said.

"You're a real wit," Katie said. "A dimwit."

Daniel raised his eyebrows. "What's your problem?"

Damita came between them. She popped a little sandwich right into Daniel's mouth. And she stayed at his side.

Katie stepped back and watched. A tape was playing and Damita tugged at Daniel to dance with her. He wouldn't, but he was laughing and they kept pulling at each other, flirting. Crystal and Leroy were standing together and talking quietly. Katie wondered what they had found to talk about. Crystal looked beautiful. It wouldn't be long before all her friends would be paired off, thought Katie. So what, she didn't need to get all twisted out of shape for any man! Not that anyone was asking her to.

There she was with her bare face hanging out, no lipstick or anything. Her arms were too long, dangling at her sides. She had nothing to do with her hands. She wished it was time to go home.

When the pizza finally came, everyone sat down at the table. Damita made Meg move over so she could take the chair next to Daniel.

"Watch out," Leroy said. "She'll give you cooties."

"Yeah," Daniel laughed, leaning away from Damita.

"Yeah, all that hair, you can't tell what's hiding in it," Eddie put in.

Damita patted her puffed-up hair. "Come on, guys, grow up," she said. She sounded so cool about it. Katie wished she could be like her.

"Oh, hey, we're grown-up," Eddie said. He dragged a pretzel through the pizza sauce and tossed it.

It bounced on Crystal's plate. "Oooh, gross," she screamed.

Meg giggled.

"Man, you missed by a mile," Daniel said.

Leroy picked a piece of sausage out of the pizza and pulled his arm back.

"No way," Damita said. "No food fight or my dad is gonna come right in here."

Katie held her hand protectively over her bow.

"What's the matter? Scared your pretty bow is gonna get dirty?" Leroy said. He reluctantly dropped the sausage back on his plate.

Katie lowered her hand.

Damita laughed. "Nice bow! What did you do, get it off a candy box?"

Katie's face got hot.

"Let me see that." Eddie fingered the bow.

"Quit it," Katie said.

He was tugging at it.

"No, don't!"

He pulled it out of her hair and waved it in the air. The bobby pins were dangling from it.

"Give it back!" Katie said. She balled up her hand, ready to punch.

Eddie leaped out of reach. "Oooh, you're scaring me!"

"Give it back!"

Leroy jumped up from the table. "Over here."

"Go get it," Eddie said as he threw it to him.

Now everyone was up. Leroy threw it to Damita.

"Give it to me!" Katie yelled. She didn't want to be monkey in the middle! She took a breath. "Come on, guys, grow up." It sounded wobbly coming out of her mouth.

Damita tossed it back to Eddie's outstretched hands.

"Stop it," Katie said. "It's my mom's!"

"Your *mama* wears baby bows?" Damita laughed.

"You keep your mouth off my mother!"

"Leave her alone," Crystal said weakly.

Katie was almost crying. The bow had been Mom's idea; Katie didn't want her to know it was all wrong. How could she explain if the bow was all messed up?

"Give it back!" Katie shouted.

"To me," Daniel said and Eddie pitched it to him.

Katie hated all of them!

Everyone was waiting for Daniel to throw. Damita had her hands out, laughing. Crystal watched, looking sad for Katie, but she wasn't doing a thing to help.

"Over here!" Leroy yelled.

Daniel looked at the bow in his hands. Then he slowly walked over to Katie and handed it to her.

She took it from him, surprised. She couldn't talk.

"What did you do that for?" Leroy asked.

Daniel looked embarrassed.

"She's a bad sport, that's all," Damita said. "It's just a dumb bow!"

Daniel cleared his throat. "No it's not. It looks pretty."

He stood there bravely, his shoulders squared, daring anybody to make fun of him. No one said anything.

Damita stared at Katie, then at Daniel, then back at Katie, studying her.

Later, when the party broke up, Daniel walked partway down the street with Katie.

"Thank you," she said. "For doing that."

He shrugged. "It's a nice bow."

"Thanks for saying that, anyway."

He hesitated. "You looked better than any of them."

She glanced at him.

"I mean it." Daniel grinned. "Who made a law that eyelids are supposed to be *green?* Where did that come from?"

Katie laughed for the first time on that long afternoon.

"So tomorrow's Sunday," Daniel said. "We've got all day to get that thing primed, okay?"

"Okay," Katie answered.

"I'll come over after church."

"Okay." It was easy to look right in his eyes and smile at him.

CHAPTER EIGHTEEN

Katie *knew* Daniel would say hi in school on Monday. They'd put the primer on the doghouse on Sunday, and Daniel even had lunch with her. Mom made her special tuna salad, with olives and hard-boiled eggs. Daniel wasn't the least bit shy with grown-ups, and Katie could tell that Mom liked him.

He was nice at Damita's party, too, in front of everybody, so Katie figured he'd say hi now. But she never thought he'd rush right over to her the way he did, the minute she came into the classroom. And she never thought it could make her so happy.

"Hey, Daniel."

He wasn't smiling, though. "You heard what happened? Somebody tried to rob the junkyard last night. There was shooting and—"

"What?" Katie felt her blood go right down to her toes. "Lucky?"

"He's not dead or nothing."

"How do you know? What happened? Are you sure Lucky—"

"I saw him when I went by this morning. Everyone was talking. There were bullet holes! They climbed over the fence and I guess they shot at Lucky, but the cops came by and they ran away and—"

"Is he *okay?*"

"I guess, but—"

Mrs. Ryan tapped her ruler on her desk. "Daniel, settle down. Get into your seat."

"Is he okay?"

"They must've missed him, but—"

"Katie! Put your coat in the closet right now. Hurry up, we're waiting for you."

Katie did as she was told. She sat down. She opened the history book to page 58 with the rest of the class. But all she could think of was Lucky. What if a bullet was in him and no one had noticed? Guarding a junkyard was too dangerous!

She had a chance to talk to Daniel again on the stairs going down to lunch.

"Could you tell he was all right? Did you see any blood on him?"

"I couldn't see that well; he was way in back of the yard. He was standing up, though. Listen, we better get that doghouse to him quick."

"What good will that do?" Katie said.

"He'd have someplace to hide."

Then Leroy called to him and Daniel caught up with his friends.

A doghouse wasn't anyplace to hide, Katie thought. Lucky would come out and bark if someone tried to break in. She knew that's what he'd do. And even if he didn't, there was that BEWARE OF DOG sign. Anybody could find him in a doghouse.

"Katie?" Crystal came up behind her.

"Oh. Hi."

"Katie, I was going to call you yesterday, but… Katie, I'm sorry about the party."

"Okay." It wasn't Crystal's fault that she wasn't brave enough to stand up for her, Katie thought. That's just the way she was. Anyway, Daniel had made it all right. But she couldn't think about the party now...

"Damita's not really mean, she was just—"

"Oh yeah? I hate her!" Katie said.

"She was just trying to be funny. She didn't think you'd get all upset."

"If you want to be friends with Damita, that's fine, but I don't—"

"She likes you. She told me."

"Sure she does."

"Damita wants a lot of attention, that's all. You should see the way it is at her house. It's like her brothers and sister are doing all interesting teenage stuff and they do all the talking and everyone forgets Damita's even there. I'm glad I'm the oldest in my family!"

"I don't care about her. She was never real friends with me."

"She wants to be now. Let's all have lunch, you, me, Damita, and Meg, like always, okay? Come on, Katie."

She let Crystal lead her to the table. It was easier than finding someone else to eat with. There was an awkward feeling. They ate their sandwiches without talking much.

Then Damita put down her ham-on-rye and said, "My party turned out pretty good. I mean, you found out Daniel likes you, right?"

Katie shrugged.

"Did he walk you home?"

"Most of the way."

"See, that proves he likes you. So that's cool!"

Katie was surprised to see Damita smiling. "I thought *you* liked him."

"Yeah, well. I don't believe in staying heart-broken. Maybe Daniel's handsome, but Eddie's the *mature* one."

Eddie, the pretzel thrower? Katie didn't say anything.

"I never thought you'd freak over that bow. You're way too thin-skinned."

"I am not!"

"Yes, you are. Listen, I'm sorry, but... you know what I would've done? I would've laughed and made a joke out of it. I would've laughed and tried to catch it."

Katie could picture Damita doing just exactly that.

"Anyway," Damita went on, "we're all going to have so much fun when we get to junior high!

I bet we'll be the most popular and…"

Damita thinks I'm "the type" now, Katie thought. All because of Daniel. The truth was, she really was getting better at talking to boys.

Later, in class, Katie looked at the back of Damita's head in the third row. She didn't one hundred percent *like* her, but she admired her. It was gutsy to give the party in the first place and invite the boys. She had been nervous about it, but she did it anyway. And Damita bounced right back when things didn't turn out right. That would be a good way to be.

But some things made Katie's heart too heavy. The way Mom would feel when Jim Grady left. And Lucky, stuck in the junkyard with no one to protect him. Daniel didn't get a good look—he could be *hurt*. The school day was dragging on much too long. Katie had to check on Lucky!

CHAPTER NINETEEN

Lucky came running as soon as he saw Katie. He seemed slower than usual. She hoped she was only imagining the limp. "Are you all right, Lucky? Does something hurt?"

He looked at her mutely, his eyes full of trust.

"You must have been so scared. I'm sorry, Lucky."

Again, she had the feeling that he was trying hard to understand her words. He cocked his head, almost frowning with concentration.

She took off her mittens and put her hands flat against the chain-link fence. He sniffed at them eagerly. She could feel the tip of his nose. It was wet; that was a good sign, wasn't it? No sign of blood on his body, not that she could see. But his coat was dirty; maybe dried blood wouldn't show.

If only there was some way she could touch him. What if there was a wound under the fur? He *was* favoring his right leg! She needed to check his paws. And she wanted to pet him. Just *pet* him!

That fence! She stretched her arms high and grabbed onto the links with her fingers. She tried to pull herself up, until her fingers were hurting and her arms seemed to be tearing from their sockets. There was no way she could get a toe-hold. The space between links was too small. Whoever had come to rob the yard last night must have had a big boost up. Or a ladder.

And they could do that again. Or someone else might. And the first thing they'd do was get rid of the guard dog.

Lucky jumped up against the fence. He tried to lick her face.

"I've almost got the doghouse done," she said, "and I'll get you a bone from Daniel's. I'll bring you an extra-good dinner tonight." But none of that made her happy anymore. The worst hurt in the world, she thought, was when you couldn't protect someone you loved.

• • • • •

It was long past dinner when Jim Grady came home that evening. Katie was finishing up her spelling homework at the kitchen table.

Jim had brought home a can of exterior paint—blue, as she'd wanted—and some pieces of carpeting.

"I cut the carpet to size," he told Katie. "Just lay it in. And there's a replacement piece for when it gets dirty."

"Uh-huh," she said.

"So all that's left is the painting. That shouldn't take long." He put the can down in the corner, next to the doghouse. "You have to let the first coat dry overnight, but you could get the whole thing finished in a couple of days."

"I saved some spaghetti for you," Mom said.

"No thanks," Jim said. "I had a good enough dinner."

"It's with that nice marinara sauce…"

"No, babe." Jim stretched. "I'm beat. I'll just wash up and hit the sack."

Mom looked disappointed. "Oh. There's a comedy special on TV. I thought we'd—"

"You go ahead, Mary Ann. Remember all the good lines for me."

"I can't tell a joke to save my life."

"Don't I know it!"

"I'm not *that* bad!" Mom said. "Well then, I guess I'll turn in, too."

"Hon, if you want to watch your show——" He yawned.

"No, it doesn't matter." Mom covered the pot and put it into the refrigerator.

She was pathetic, Katie thought. Practically begging him to eat her spaghetti. And going to bed at ten o'clock! She'd do *anything* to be with him.

Jim started out of the kitchen. Then he turned back toward Katie. "When does Farrow come to the yard?"

"Mostly Thursdays and Saturdays."

"Okay, I'll carry it over with you on Saturday."

"All right," Katie said.

Jim smiled. "Well, looks like you did it! All by yourself."

Katie didn't smile back. Jim looked at her, puzzled.

The smell of garlic and oregano still hung in the air.

"Well, good night," he said.

"Good night," she mumbled. She had to make up a sentence for each spelling word. In her loose-leaf notebook she wrote, "Her efforts were *ineffectual*."

Jim was leaning in the doorway, looking at her. "What's the matter? I can't take off Thursday. Another couple of days won't make a difference."

"The whole doghouse won't make a difference!"

"Katie's upset," Mom said. "Someone tried to break into the junkyard. Sweetie, nothing happened. That dog will be just fine."

"You don't know that. How would you know? You're always saying things are just fine when they're not."

"Don't get fresh," Jim said.

Katie clenched her fists. "Don't tell me what to do!"

"All right now," Mom said. "Settle down. Everything will look better in the morning... You want to shower first?"

"You go ahead," Jim said. "I'm gonna talk to Katie a minute."

"All this about a junkyard dog." Mom sighed as she left the kitchen.

Jim waited until she was out of earshot. "Why take it out on your mama? It's not her fault."

"Nothing's going to be better in the morning. Not a single thing."

"Look, you've been feeding him. As of Saturday, he'll have a shelter. You're getting him through the winter."

"So what?" Katie said. "He's filthy. No one ever pets him. No one knows if he's hurt or not. He's out there all night, and anybody can come along and shoot at him or do anything they want to him. All I'm doing is keeping him alive for a while." Tears welled up in her eyes. "He's got an awful life. He doesn't deserve that."

Jim listened quietly.

"Kids throw things at him. Mr. Farrow yells at him. Probably hits him. Nothing's gonna be better for him, no matter what I do. The doghouse is no big deal."

The chair creaked as Jim sat down. Katie could hear the water running in the bathroom.

"I think he's limping," she said.

"Maybe..." Jim said.

"What?"

"I didn't want to get your hopes up before. I don't make promises I can't keep."

Right, Katie thought. Staying married was a promise that he wouldn't be keeping.

"It might be a lot different in the spring because—"

"Why?" asked Katie. "You planning to move on in the spring?"

"What?"

"Then why don't you *go?* What are you hanging around for? It only makes it worse for Mom."

"Whoa, what's that all about? What's 'worse'?"

"It was bad enough one man took off on her and now you... Oh, never mind." Katie riffled the pages of her notebook. "I don't care."

"What? You think I'm taking off?"

"Well, aren't you?"

"No!" he exploded.

Katie stared at him, startled.

His jaw was set hard. "So that's what you think of me?"

Katie shrugged.

"I love your mother. Get used to it; no one's prying me loose!" He shoved his chair back from the table with a loud scrape and stood up, furious. "What's going on in that head? You think I'm planning a disappearing act like your fly-by-night father?"

"Don't you talk about my father!" Jim Grady had no business badmouthing her family!

"I don't appreciate being lumped in that group. I'd appreciate more respect than that. Look at me and you're looking at a *man*. I'm no punk weaseling out with the last of the grocery money and not even a carton of milk in—"

"He was too young, that's all. Mom said."

"Sure. Mary Ann was even younger, wasn't she?" He was blazing mad. "You're only eleven and you're taking care of that dog, aren't you? More than he did for his own kid."

"That's not so!"

"Then where is he?"

Katie bit her lip hard. Jim Grady didn't need to be so mean! It was all she could do not to cry.

A long, long silence ticked by. Jim turned and paced away. He stared at the humming refrigerator. Then he faced Katie and came toward her.

"Sorry," he finally said. "I guess I shouldn't have…" He pulled the chair back and sank down. "All right, where did you get the idea I'm leaving?"

Katie scraped her fingernail along the table edge.

He leaned across the table. "What did I do? Did I say something? Come on, what?"

"I heard you yelling and fighting and… You said you wanted to get outta here, remember, the way you were going on about trees and a backyard? And you took all that overtime, you come back later every night and——" Katie caught her breath. "You *said* you were moving on."

He sighed. "You don't have a bit of trust, do you?"

"Well, that's what you *said,* right to my face."

"I meant *us* moving on." He ran his fingers through his hair. "I expected you'd know that."

"How'm I supposed to know what you mean?" Maybe he just didn't want to admit it, not right then, not to her. "*Us?* I don't know what you're talking about."

Jim shook his head. "You can't go ahead and think all men are the same, just because——"

"He was *nice,*" Katie said. "Mom *told* me."

Jim was looking hard at her. She looked at the wall, at the kitchen cabinets, every which way but in his eyes.

They both listened to the shower running.

"White-lie excuses get you all mixed up," Jim said. "Everyone's *not* the same, you need to know that. You'll need to know what to look for when you're old enough for a man of your own. Someone who'll follow through on his promises, no excuses, and take responsibility. Any less ain't good enough."

He was speaking the truth about that, Katie thought.

"I started to tell you before. About in the spring."

He sounded as though there was something big on his mind. Katie held her breath, ready for bad news.

"I had my mind set on *us* moving. Why do you think I'm putting in all that overtime? You think I like it?"

"I don't know what you like."

"There's a block over in Huntsville with little houses and front yards. Trees all along the street. There's a handyman special that I can fix up till it shines."

All he'd been doing was daydreaming out loud about moving to some house. I'd gotten him all wrong, Katie thought. She guessed she owed him an apology; it gave her a bad, squirmy feeling.

"Now don't start thinking it's some mansion, but...we're just about ready for a down payment on it."

Katie sat up straight. "What?" This was for real! "Where did you say?"

"Huntsville. Listen, next time you don't understand what's going on, ask me and I'll tell you straight out. Okay?"

Huntsville! What about her friends? How could she watch out for Lucky from way over in Huntsville? "That's too far!"

"It's still within city limits, just down the river. No more than a bus ride away, so your mom and I will be going to work in the other direction, that's all."

No one had even checked with her! It made her so mad that she almost didn't catch his next words.

"And you can have a dog. In our house, we'll be the ones making the rules."

Her heart skipped a beat. "Lucky? Can I have Lucky?"

"That's what I'm thinking."

"'Cause I wouldn't want any other dog," she said cautiously.

"I know."

"We'll get him out of the junkyard?" It was the best thing that could ever happen! "He'll be so happy! He'll be my dog?" It was too good to be true.

"I can't see any reason Farrow wouldn't let him go. He can always get a replacement. Listen, we'll throw him a few bucks if we need to."

Katie jumped up and almost hugged Jim

before she caught herself. "I can't believe it! I'd take such good care of him. I would."

Jim nodded.

She could hardly stand still. She was flooded with sunshine right down to her toes.

They heard the bathroom door open and then Mom's footsteps in the bedroom. "Jim?" she called. "All yours."

"Be right there," he called. He got up and stretched. "Better finish up that homework."

As if she could think about spelling now!

Jim was halfway through the doorway, filling up the space and silhouetted by the hall bulb.

"I could help you with that house," Katie said. "Doing carpentry and stuff."

He turned back. "That would be nice."

CHAPTER TWENTY

All night long, different pictures were running through her mind, like pieces of a movie. She saw herself bathing Lucky and he was splashing until they were both soaked and she was laughing so hard. Then she was brushing him out until his fur was soft and beautiful and glowing golden. She was running with him in the grass. She was throwing a stick and he got it and brought it back and barked for her to play some more. Then her arms were around him and he was resting his head against her, all warm and peaceful.

Huntsville. A room all her own would be good, but she didn't know anybody in Huntsville. Not a soul. She hoped it wasn't tough, with lots of gangs. It *had* to be nice; Jim

Grady wouldn't move them to a bad place... But she'd be going to a different school. Junior high, without Crystal or Meg, or even Damita. Without Daniel kind of liking her. Something squeezed her stomach.

She couldn't imagine living anyplace else but the Mud Flats. She loved the bustle at Palmer Square. The big old movie house. The vendors with trays of woodcarvings and beads from far away, talking fast in a different language. Music drifting from the stores and live music right there on the corner, the day some black boys were playing steel drums and she and Crystal danced along on the sidewalk. Devil's Run—it was the best sledding hill in the world. The new Ben and Jerry's—she hadn't even been there yet! P.A.L. basketball—she was getting good, too! She knew everyone in church, old people and kids; after the singing, they'd be greeting each other so warm and respectful: "Good morning, Mrs. Leonetti." "And how are you today, Miz Lawrence?" The Mud Flats was home. She didn't know anything else.

But then happiness bubbled up again. They'd be like a TV family in a house—her, Mom, Jim Grady, and Lucky. Jim Grady would be there to take care of things. Maybe there'd be roses climbing up a trellis... In the new school, she'd get everyone to call her Katherine. That was more grown-up than Katie. She'd have *attitude* and...

It got all mixed up in her dreams as she finally drifted off to sleep.

In school, Mrs. Ryan kept them busy with tests all morning. Katie didn't have a chance to tell Daniel. His seat was way on the other side of the room.

At recess, Katie saw him leaning against the red-brick wall. He was by himself for a minute; she rushed right over.

"Guess what happened? I'm going to get Lucky!"

"You winning the lottery or what?"

"Lucky! The dog! He'll be mine, for real."

"How come? I thought you couldn't—"

"I can now, 'cause we'll be moving. So I can get him out of the junkyard! He'll have a real home."

"He sure needs one. You're moving out of the projects?"

Katie nodded.

"Where to?"

"Huntsville. Not until the spring, though. Lucky still has to get through the winter."

"He'll have the doghouse. Good thing it didn't snow again."

"Jim Grady brought paint home last night. That's all we have to do, and then it's done."

"We could paint this afternoon," Daniel said.

"Okay. If I can keep him healthy until spring...and then, he'll be so happy!"

"Fresh meat's good for dogs. I'll save all the scraps."

Leroy passed by and pulled Daniel's jacket sleeve. "Let's go."

"Hey, you guys playing ball or not?" Eddie called from under the hoops.

"I'll be there in a minute," Daniel said.

"Daniel's with *Katie,*" Leroy said in falsetto. He ran onto the court.

Daniel got busy fiddling with the zipper on his jacket.

"Yo!" Eddie shouted. "What're you waiting for?"

Katie saw Daniel take a breath. There was just a second of hesitation before he called back, "Later! Can't you see I'm talking to somebody?"

They watched Leroy run to the court and steal the ball from Eddie. Then John blocked him and two other boys were there, too, and someone was jumping for a shot.

"That's okay," Katie said softly. "Go ahead if you want to."

"I want to ask you something," Daniel said. "Where's Huntsville?"

"Down the river."

"Oh."

"Jim Grady's buying a house."

"Oh." He scuffed his sneaker along the pavement. "That's good news, huh?"

"I guess," Katie said. "Well, it sure is for Lucky!"

"How do you know Farrow's gonna let you have him?"

"He doesn't care anything about Lucky. He can always get another dog."

"Yeah, if he gives you a hard time, you could pay him something."

"Another dog," Katie said slowly. "That means another dog in Lucky's spot."

"Yeah, well... At least Lucky's out of there."

"Another junkyard dog. He'll be miserable. He'll be hungry and scared."

"You can't take in every single stray," Daniel said.

"I know, but it makes me feel awful."

"Yeah," Daniel said. "They have a tough time."

"It seems like rescuing Lucky won't do that much good."

"Except for Lucky. For him, it's a miracle."

"I know. I'm happy about that part, but…"

Katie heard the chant of the girls jumping double Dutch. She heard the basketball thumping on the cement. It was too cold to be standing still for long.

"Tell you what," Daniel said. "If Farrow puts another dog in there, I'll help him out."

"You will?"

"Like you did with Lucky. I'll bring him food and water."

Katie studied his face. "Will you remember?"

"I just said so, didn't I?"

He would, she thought. He'd remember.

Daniel grinned. "I'll name him Thunder."

Katie smiled. "And I won't be here to make you change it." Not be here—it was hard to imagine. She started to bite her lip, but remembered not to; that's what made her lips get chapped all winter. "Anyway, it won't be until spring. That's a long way off."

"Maybe—" Daniel started. Then he got real interested in a pebble on the ground.

Katie watched him and waited.

"Maybe when you're in Huntsville, I'll call

you once in a while. To find out how Lucky's getting along."

"It's not that far. Only a bus ride. So you could come over sometimes." Katie stuck her hands into her pockets. "I mean, to see Lucky."

"Sure, I'll come see Lucky. See how he's doing."

"You won't recognize him, I bet. He'll be looking good."

"Okay, that's cool," Daniel said. He nodded as if something had been settled.

"Hey, Daniel!" That was John. "We need you, man!"

"We'll talk later, all right?" Daniel said.

"Sure," Katie said. "Go ahead." Maybe in her new school, *girls* played basketball at recess, too. Or maybe she'd be the one to get that started...

She watched Daniel run to the court. She watched him play for a while. All his moves looked graceful to her.

Daniel is one of the responsible ones, she thought.

CHAPTER TWENTY-ONE

Katie and Jim Grady passed an old lady feeding the pigeons. She was sitting on her bench outside the project's playground. "Good afternoon, Mr. Grady."

"How are you today, Miz Cornell?" Jim said. He shifted the doghouse on his shoulder. It was shiny with fresh blue paint.

"Feeling my arthritis in this weather," she said. "Soon as it starts freezing up."

Jim nodded. "It sure is cold."

Katie could feel the icy wind creeping under her jacket as they walked along the street. She pulled her collar up around her neck.

"Lucky's getting his house just in time," Katie said. She couldn't stop looking at it. It looked *good*—and she had made it! She felt like she could do anything, even in Huntsville, even in a new school.

Jim glanced at her. "Your ears are gonna fall off. Where's that cap of yours?"

"I guess maybe I might have lost it." The rabbit hat was tucked at the bottom of her drawer. She hadn't had the heart to throw it out because it was handmade by Grandma Hattie.

"Where'd you lose it?"

"I can't wear it anyway. It's too dumb."

"What's wrong with it?"

"No one my age wears bunnies!" Sometimes Jim Grady didn't know a thing.

"It has bunnies on it?"

"Yes!"

"Oh," he said.

They turned the corner at St. Francis Street.

Jim raised his eyebrows. "So you *lost* it, huh? You ought to have something on your head. Tell your mom to get you a new one."

"You said she shouldn't."

"I did?"

"Yes."

"Oh. Hmmmm. Well, you got to remember, I'm still learning about kids." He smiled. "Go ahead and get yourself a new one."

Katie thought for a long moment. "It's all right," she finally said. "We can save the money for the down payment."

His smile broadened. "Thanks, Katie, but we'll manage a new cap. That's pretty important."

Katie looked up at him. He hadn't shaved. He looked tired and grizzly in the pale sunlight. Saturday was his day for sleeping. "Thanks for taking the doghouse."

"There's no way you could carry it," he said. "Anyway, I want to have a word with Farrow."

They reached the junkyard. Good, Katie thought, Mr. Farrow was there. Lucky ran to the fence.

"Hello!" Jim called.

Farrow approached. He squinted at them. "Yeah?"

"We want to bring the doghouse in."

"What doghouse?" Farrow looked at it on Jim's shoulder. "What's that for?"

"For the dog!" Katie said impatiently. "I made it. You *said* I could put it in the yard."

Farrow looked at both of them as though they were crazy. "You made that thing?" He slowly unlocked the door.

"Thanks," Jim said.

As soon as Katie stepped into the yard, Lucky

jumped at her. His front paws slid on her jacket. He smelled doggy. His tail was wagging double-time.

"Down, mutt!" Farrow yelled.

"Let them be," Jim said.

Katie had never been able to pet him before. She took off her mittens and he licked her hands. His tongue was warm and wet; she just managed to keep her face out of his reach. His fur felt springy on top and soft underneath. His body wriggled ecstatically as she petted him. It was exactly the way she had imagined. He went round and round her feet in excited circles.

"I guess this should go in back," Jim said.

Katie nodded.

"I don't need more clutter," Farrow mumbled. He followed them to the back of the yard. When Jim put the doghouse down, Farrow eyed it and ran his hand along the roof.

"Here's your house, Lucky," Katie said.

The dog didn't look at it. His body was pressed against her legs.

"He doesn't like it," Katie said, dismayed.

"Don't worry," Jim said. "He'll make good use of it; right now, he's busy with you."

Katie scratched his head and behind his ears. His ears were like velvet. He nudged her hand with his nose. Every move of his body showed his craving for affection; it almost broke her heart.

"Okay, you brought it in," Farrow said. "I don't have all day."

"Please, give us a minute with the dog," Jim said. "You can go ahead and do whatever."

Jim Grady towered over Mr. Farrow. Farrow looked up at him. He started to say something, changed his mind, and grumbled as he moved away.

Katie was running her hands through Lucky's coat. "I don't feel anything, but would you check?"

As Jim bent down, Lucky backed away. He stood stiff-legged, on guard.

"It's okay," Katie said. "This is Jim Grady. He's nice."

"All right, boy," Jim said. "Easy, boy."

Gradually, Lucky relaxed. He allowed Jim to touch him.

"There's nothing," Jim said. "He's okay."

"I still think he's favoring his right leg."

"Good dog," Jim said softly as he lifted the dog's paw. "You were right, Katie. He's got something stuck between the pads."

"Is he cut? What is it? Is he hurt?"

"Here." Jim held up a tiny piece of metal. It glinted in the sun. "I don't think it cut in; his leather's pretty tough. It must've been uncomfortable, though."

"I can't wait to get him out of here!"

"He's been lucky so far," he said, "and spring's not that far off."

Jim waited as Katie stroked Lucky again and again. She wanted to make up for all his long lonely time.

Mr. Farrow kept looking over at them.

"I think we have to go," Jim said.

Reluctantly, Katie followed Jim. Lucky trailed alongside; his eyes were begging her not to leave him behind. She bent down to scratch him one last time. "Soon," she whispered.

Mr. Farrow unlocked the door.

"Just one thing," Jim said to him. "Just so it's real clear. That doghouse is Katie's property. It's here for the dog—on loan."

Farrow's eyes shifted away from Jim's. "Yeah, yeah."

"Don't even think about selling it off or you'll be answering to me."

"I'm not selling nothing," Farrow mumbled. He didn't look so fierce when he was talking to Jim.

"All right then." Jim put out his hand. "My name's Grady."

Farrow shrugged and shook his hand.

"I appreciate your courtesy to Katie."

Farrow looked from one to the other. "What is she, your daughter?"

"That's right," Jim said.

When they were on the street and out of earshot, Katie said, "You didn't tell him we want Lucky."

"Not yet. Not till we're ready to take him."

"You said I was your daughter."

"Seemed simpler than an explanation. I want him to know I'll be around."

They waited to cross the street. A car passed, blasting rap into the air.

"Do you mind?" he asked.

Katie could hardly hear him with all the noise. "What?"

"My saying you're my daughter?"

"No, I don't mind. It's…it's simpler."

They went across the street and up the block. Without the weight of the doghouse on his shoulder, Jim Grady walked too fast.

"When we move," he said, "you'll be going to a new school."

"I know."

"It might be simpler to register you as Katie Grady. Same name as your mother, so there's less confusion."

"Okay," Katie said. "Less confusion that way."

"That means I'd be adopting you," he said.

For the first time since she'd known him, he didn't look so sure of himself. She felt him studying her face.

"Legally." He paused. "Does that sound all right to you?"

"That sounds all right," Katie said softly.

They were going past the playground. Mrs. Cornell was still out. The flock of pigeons was gathered around her. A few fluttered away as they went by.

"You're walking too fast for me," Katie said.

"Sorry, never had a daughter before."

Katie looked up at him quickly. He smiled. She smiled back.

"What should I call you?" Katie asked.

"Whatever feels comfortable."

She thought for a moment. "Is 'Jim' all right?"

He nodded. "That's fine."

That felt comfortable for now, Katie thought.

She tucked her mittened hand into his as they went up the path to the building.